In the blink of an eye, a fu
Experience enabled Shane to
truck before it jackknifed, his
precariously on the back. Above ... screech of the truck's brakes locking, a blood-curdling scream sliced through the very core of his being.

Shane dropped his bike, lunged forward, and rounded the back of the truck in the same instant his wife and her bike parted ways. He heard the resounding crunch of metal as her Ironhead bounced off the cab and tumbled down the side of the mountain. Kelly flew through the haze of dirt and debris, landed with a sickening crunch; her body slid down the road.

"Kelly!" Shane ran wildly after his wife. Sliding on his knees, he caught her crumpled body and held her head on his lap. Her glazed eyes held his for the briefest of moments before rolling back, her lids closing for the last time.

"Somebody help! You fucking bastard! You rotten, mother fucking, son of a bitch!"

Shane's venomous outburst stopped the dazed driver who burst from the passenger side of the truck. The man turned and stumbled back to call for help. A spasm of coughing stopped Shane's tirade. The acrid stench of diesel fuel assaulted his senses. Sobbing, Shane brushed his wife's matted curls from her bruised and bloodied face. Hearing the familiar rumble of a motorcycle, Shane looked up to see a man wearing a wide-brimmed leather hat come out from behind the truck. The stranger crouched down beside his bike and tied something to his swing arm.

"Hey! Over here!" Shane waved his hand in the air.

Shane rubbed his burning eyes with the heel of his hand, only to see the man was no longer there. Teetering on the brink of hysteria, Shane covered Kelly's mouth with his own. He blew long and hard in a futile attempt to fill her lungs with his breath. Gasping, he buried his face in her blonde curls, desperate to inhale her very essence.

Visit Adelle Laudan at:
http://www.adellelaudan.com/
http://www.myspace.com/adellelaudan

If you enjoyed this book, you may also wish to read:

Bad Things by J.G. Craig
Dark Roads & The Boy in the Grey Tracksuit by J.G. Craig
Decimate: A Horror Anthology by Various Authors
Fade to Pale by James Cheetham
Odd Pursuits by Robert Castle
Oh, Ragnarok! By Gabrielle Llana
Pervalism by M.E. Ellis
Quits: Book 1: Demons by M.E. Ellis
Quits: Book 2: Devils by M.E. Ellis
Shutterbug by Daniel I. Russell
Soul Haven by Sonja Baines

And come chat with Wild Child authors at:
Wild Child Authors Yahoo group:
http://groups.yahoo.com/group/wcp_authors/

Wild Child Publishing Yahoo group:
http://groups.yahoo.com/group/wildchildpublishingchat/

Or stay up to date with what is happening at WCP:

WCP/FB News Blog: http://wcpfbnews.blogspot.com/
WCP MySpace Page: http://www.myspace.com/wildchildpublishing

Iron Horse Rider
by
Adelle Laudan

Wishing You Miles of Smiles
Adelle Laudan
2007

Wild Child Publishing.com
Culver City, California

Iron Horse Rider
Copyright © 2007
by Adelle Laudan

Cover illustration by Wild Child Publishing © 2007
For information on the cover art, please contact covervan@aol.com.

All rights reserved. No part of this book may be reproduced or transmitted in any form without written permission from the publisher, except by a reviewer who may quote brief passages for review purposes.

This book is a work of fiction and any resemblance to any person, living or dead, any place, events or occurrences, is purely coincidental. The characters and story lines are created from the author's imagination or are used fictitiously.

Editor: Faith Bicknell-Brown

ISBN: 1-934069- 51-5 – ebook
ISBN: 1-934069-54-X – paperback

Wild Child Publishing.com
P.O. Box 4897
Culver City, CA 90231-4897

Printed in The United States of America

Dedicated
To
Brutus

Together we ride life's twist and turns
Together creating memories in the wind
Together we will grow old
Living...
Loving...
Laughing...

Together

RIDING IN THE RAIN

*Some folks ride in the rain
To wash away their tears
Yearning for days of yesterday
Never shifting gears*

*They always ride the same old roads
Never venturing into the unknown
Cursing their life for opportunities missed
Crying as they head home*

*I don't dwell on days gone by
I took a different route
I look forward to the open skies,
Riding free is what it's all about*

*So, I bring to life my iron beast
As quickly as can be
I don't want to miss a moment in time
There's still too much left to see*

*I want to feel the winds of time
Blowing in my face
I want to find many new roads
Not happy to be just taking up space*

*I want to see what's up ahead
Not where I should have turned
Life's too short to have regrets
Just long enough to learn*

*So when the rain is upon us
When you hear the thunder crack
Go for a ride and cleanse your spirit
Get your life back on track*

It's all right to walk down memory lane,
That's part of who we are
But, today is for the living
To chase a shooting star

The thrill is in the mystery
Not what you already know
In the wind is where it's happening
Not knowing where you go

Life is riding all the twists and turns
Even when it starts to rain
It's living in the moment
Ride on or go insane

You can't see what's around every corner
Sometimes you have to make a change
The world is yours for the taking
Even when it means riding in the rain

Adelle Laudan
Copyright © 2004

Chapter One

In the blink of an eye, a fully loaded log truck veered into their path. Experience enabled Shane to maneuver his motorcycle around the truck before it jackknifed, his vision blocked by the load of logs swaying precariously on the back. Above the screech of the truck's brakes locking, a blood-curdling scream sliced through the very core of his being.

Shane dropped his bike, lunged forward, and rounded the back of the truck in the same instant his wife and her bike parted ways. He heard the resounding crunch of metal as her Ironhead bounced off the cab and tumbled down the side of the mountain. Kelly flew through the haze of dirt and debris, landed with a sickening crunch; her body slid down the road.

"Kelly!" Shane ran wildly after his wife. Sliding on his knees, he caught her crumpled body and held her head on his lap. Her glazed eyes held his for the briefest of moments before rolling back, her lids closing for the last time.

"Somebody help! You fucking bastard! You rotten, mother fucking, son of a bitch!"

Shane's venomous outburst stopped the dazed driver who burst from the passenger side of the truck. The man turned and stumbled back to call for help. A spasm of coughing stopped Shane's tirade. The acrid stench of diesel fuel assaulted his senses. Sobbing, Shane brushed his wife's matted curls from her bruised and bloodied face. Hearing the familiar rumble of a motorcycle, Shane looked up to see a man wearing a wide-brimmed leather hat come out from behind the truck. The stranger crouched down beside his bike and tied something to his swing arm.

"Hey! Over here!" Shane waved his hand in the air.

Shane rubbed his burning eyes with the heel of his hand, only to see the man was no longer there. Teetering on the brink of hysteria, Shane covered Kelly's mouth with his own. He blew long and hard in a futile attempt to fill her lungs with his breath. Gasping, he buried his face in her blonde curls, desperate to inhale her very essence.

The darkness erupted in a whirl of sirens and flashing lights. An attendant bolted from the rescue truck and fell to his knees next to Shane. He placed his hand gingerly on her limp wrist in search of a pulse. Finding none, the EMT sadly affirmed what he already knew with a nod. Shane hung his head. Slowly, he gathered his wife to his chest.

Another onslaught of blaring sirens signaled the arrival of an ambulance. The attendant beside Shane jumped up and halted their approach. After confirming Kelly's demise, two men pulled a stretcher from the back of the ambulance and jogged over to where she lay crumpled on the road. One of the attendants placed a hand cautiously on Shane's shoulder. He looked up in despair, allowing the other EMT to take Kelly from him and place her on the waiting stretcher. He took a white sheet and covered her broken body. Before the man had finished with her death shroud, Shane pulled the sheet away from her face and lovingly tucked it up under her chin. Puzzled, the young attendant looked at him.

"She doesn't like anything over her face while she sleeps." His voice cracked.

The attendant simply nodded, and the two men lifted the stretcher, placing her in the back of the ambulance. Shane stood in the middle of the road, his hands hanging limply at his sides, vaguely aware of the scene before him.

The police arrived and exchanged a few words with the shaken trucker before placing him in the back of their car. One of the officers brushed against Shane as he eased up next to him. Lethal rage gurgled in the pit of his stomach as he listened to him say the driver had fallen asleep behind the wheel. Without making a conscious decision, he flung himself against the door of the cruiser, screaming obscenities at the driver. Two officers pulled him back and didn't let go of him until another cruiser showed up to take the man away.

Shane insisted that he leave on his bike. He straddled his motorcycle and looked over the road's edge. There, he spotted Kelly's Ironhead wrapped around a tree growing between the deep ravines on the mountainside.

"I want her bike," he said, his eyes trained on the wreckage. "If you can't do it, I know a group of guys who can."

The officer nodded. "It'll be taken care of. I don't think you should be riding, so why don't you let us take you home? We'll make sure your bike is safe."

"It ain't gonna happen." Shane started his bike.

"I'll be right behind you," said the officer and walked towards his cruiser.

Shane shrugged and kicked his bike to life. He took one last look back, twisted the throttle, and gunned it down the road. He rode everywhere and nowhere until the sun crept up over the mountain. The whole time, the cruiser followed at a safe distance.

After hours of riding aimlessly, exhaustion seeped into his bones and began to take its toll on his body. *Where do I go? Home?* He tilted his head back and let out an ironic laugh. *Home, they just took my home away on a stretcher. How can I ever set foot in our house again?* In the wee hours of the morning, Shane found himself in front of the Clubhouse. There were half a dozen bikes out front, but he didn't want to go in there. He'd go to the shop instead. It'd be the last place they'd look for him on a nice day.

Shane got off his ride and swung the door back, rolling his Shovel inside and locking the door behind him. Once inside, he stumbled over to the old wood stove to start a fire. He stuffed kindling inside, reached out for a small log, and stopped, his hand in midair. *Where there's smoke, there's fire. If the boys see smoke, they'll know I'm here.* With his heart heavy, Shane dropped the log and trudged over to his chair in a dark corner of the shop.

He laid his head against the back of the chair. Drawing his knees up to his chest, he closed his eyes. A small smile played on his lips; tears rolled from his weary eyes as he remembered the day he'd first laid eyes on Kelly.

* * *

On Shane's thirtieth birthday, his adopted family of misfit bikers insisted on throwing him a party. He'd been standing at the window in his shop, mesmerized by the virgin snow drifting down from an ominous gray sky.

He rubbed the goose bumps covering his bare arms. How long had he been standing at the window? He walked over to an old cast-iron stove. Every time he heard the door's annoying screech, it reminded him he should oil the hinges. Shane threw a few sticks and another log on the dwindling fire and closed the door tight. He rubbed his hands together over the grate.

"Holy shit it's cold!" The door opened with a burst of frigid air and Tommy stomped into the shop.

Shane looked over and laughed at Tommy's cherry red nose and long dark mane dusted with snow. *Bikers sure don't fare well in the cold and snowy months of winter.*

"What the hell are you still doing here?" Tommy took off his gloves. "You don't think you're getting out of your party, do you?"

"Don't get your shit in a knot." Shane chuckled. "I got plenty of time, don't I?"

"If you call half an hour plenty of time, I guess you do." Tommy edged past bike parts and stood by the stove, his nicotine-stained teeth chattering as he talked.

"No shit?" replied Shane. "I guess it's a good thing you stopped in. It'd be a crying shame if I missed the party." He failed to hide the sarcasm in his voice. He hated being the center of attention, but the only thing he hated more was obnoxious drunks getting in his face. Some of the other brothers tended to tip the bottle too much at such get-togethers. They'd either end up in a fight or slobbering over anyone who'd listen to their sad stories.

"Do what you like, brother." Tommy scowled, his brow rising suspiciously. "I can always find a home for the Keenan carburetor elsewhere."

"Hey now, a deal's a deal." Tommy punched his friend on the arm. "I expect *my* sweet carb to magically appear on this workbench by morning."

Tommy shook his head. "Pretty bad when you have to bribe a person to go to their own goddamn birthday party!"

Both men laughed.

Another gust of cold air swirled through the shop. The massive frame of their brother, Barry, stood in the doorway.

"Ho, ho, fucking ho!" His deep baritone voice filled the shop. "Who the fuck ordered this white shit anyway?"

Barry stepped into the cluttered room and pulled a small blonde woman from his shadow. She stood next to him shivering, her face flushed. The odd wisp of honey blonde hair curled up and kissed her cheeks, sparkling with a light dusting of snow.

"This is Rita's sister, Kelly. Meet Shane and Tommy," the big man's voice rumbled. He pulled a bandana from his worn leather jacket to wipe the sheen from his baldhead.

Shane turned, feeling his throat constrict at the sight of the woman before him. He marveled at the overwhelming urge to push back a stray golden ringlet covering one of her powder blue eyes. He imagined her skin soft as brushed deerskin as his hand lingered against her glowing cheeks. Shane's mother left a sour taste in his mouth when it came to women. Once a beautiful woman in her own right, she could now be seen stumbling down Main Street after spending all day on a bar stool. Sure, he liked women well enough; he just rarely let them get too close.

Shane grunted a hello and sat down on a stool in front of his bike he'd named Belle. *It ain't happening lady, you can bat them baby blues some place else.* He picked up a wrench and started taking off the bolts that held his seat in place and dropped them with a clink into a rusted coffee tin. He saw the glares Barry and Tommy aimed in his direction. Heavy tension hung in the shop.

Kelly shot questioning looks at Tommy and her brother-in-law.

Tommy moved over to her side and put his arm around her tiny waist. "Pay no attention to Mr. Congeniality here. Let me buy you a drink next door."

Kelly pursed her heart-shaped lips, looking confused. She seemed even smaller than she was, standing between the two bikers. Barry took one of his gloves and smacked Shane upside the head and slammed the door shut behind him.

Shane let out a long, relieved breath. He dropped the wrench and stood. Throwing on his black leather jacket and flinging a long knit scarf around his neck, he braced himself against the swirl of snow that would twirl around his long legs outside. Luckily, the house he shared with a few of the guys sat just beyond the driveway.

Later, after he'd showered and changed, he found himself taking extra care in trimming his goatee and mustache. He finished with a liberal splash of aftershave on his smooth face before looking himself in the eye. *The only person you're fooling is yourself, asshole.* Try as he might, he couldn't erase the vision of her from his thoughts, or come up with one logical reason she'd be different from the rest. Shrugging at his reflection, he turned and left the bathroom. He took the stairs two at a time, jumped down the last three steps, and landed with a thud at the bottom. Shane put on his riding boots and tucked his long, shiny hair inside the neck of his leather coat as he slipped out the door.

Very aware of the monster lurking in every liquor bottle, Shane rarely drank. Usually, when a party kicked into high gear, he'd slip out the back door. He knew all too well his lack of tolerance for drunks so he figured it best if he just left rather than stick around to end up in a fistfight later.

Pickups and cars littered the parking lot. Shane grimaced at the thought of having to go inside. Maybe if he snuck in the back he could avoid the whole Happy Birthday ordeal. He trudged around back through the snow to discover the rear entrance locked.

"Fuck!" He crossed the yard to the shop, only to find himself locked out of it too. Shane kicked the door, and a heavy blanket of snow tumbled down on his head. With a clenched fist he drew back to punch the door, but thought better of it when he looked up and saw the remaining snow. He unzipped his coat in a futile attempt to stop the snow from further melting down his back.

Thoroughly pissed off, he stomped over to the front door of the clubhouse and opened it. Greeted by wall-to-wall bikers erupting in a collective shout of Happy Birthday, Shane shook his head in despair and headed for the bar.

Every impulse in his body cried out for a shot of liquid courage. He forced the desire from his mind and scanned the room. A gaggle of old ladies flocked around him with Birthday wishes. He reluctantly stooped to receive kisses, feeling extremely uncomfortable as the center of attention. He turned to find his usual mug of coffee sitting on the bar in front of him.

"Can I buy you a shot for your birthday?" The scruffy-faced bartender smiled a toothless grin and pushed a shot glass filled to capacity towards him.

"Coffee's fine, thanks." Shane raised his mug in cheers while the bartender lifted the shot intended for him and knocked it back.

Music blared so loudly that Shane grimaced. A huge array of food covered the capped pool table. In the center sat a massive cake with an artistically iced bike under the blue icing that spelled out Happy Birthday. Shane couldn't remember his last birthday cake. A couple of the regular girls from the Clubhouse firmly planted themselves on each side of him. Regardless, he found himself searching the crowded room for Kelly.

The room thinned out as the night progressed, offering him an empty barstool. Much to his surprise, he turned to the seat next to his to find Kelly nursing a cup of coffee. He looked at her boldly and reveled in the intoxicating depth of her alluring blue eyes.

"Happy Birthday," she said, matching his gaze.

"Thanks. How's your coffee?"

"Cold." Kelly frowned. In contrast, her blue eyes sparkled.

"Can I buy you a drink?"

"If you're offering a fresh *hot* coffee, I'd love one."

Pleased with her answer, Shane excused himself and rounded the bar to put on a fresh pot. The bartender had long ago disappeared, leaving Shane to serve a few drinks. By the time he finished, the coffee pot let out a final gurgle. He filled two clean mugs and returned to his seat. Kelly sat with her feet up on his barstool, saving his spot.

Shane found himself talking about things normally deemed off limits. In exchange, he learned about her alcoholic father.

"After my father rode off on his blue Indian, my mother developed a love affair with the whiskey bottle."

"That must've been tough on you, especially at so young an age," said Kelly, sympathy in her eyes.

He shrugged. "I learned to deal with it."

In the wee hours of the morning, he warmed up his truck and drove her back to Barry's. Sitting out front of the house, Shane struggled with himself not to kiss her. He couldn't allow himself to fall for her. He said a curt good-bye, ignoring the puzzled expression on her face as she climbed out of the truck.

Days after his birthday party, Shane realized with dismay that he'd spent as much time with Kelly as possible. The fact that he felt as though he'd known her forever both delighted and frightened him. She was easy to talk to and a ready listener, so finding himself talking to her about anything and everything rattled him as well. Inevitably, Kelly announced she had to return home, and the bottom fell out of Shane's heart.

He struggled to maintain the façade and feigned indifference while listening to her. Watching her lip tremble with disappointment almost broke him, but he convinced himself they were both better off parting way**s**.

They drove to the station in silence. Shane carried her bag inside and waited off to one side while she checked in. As she closed the distance between them, the intercom buzzed with the announcement her train was boarding. She'd quickened her pace, reaching up to cover his mouth with her lips in a hungry urgency. Shane instinctively pulled away, but stopped short and gave into the governing impulse to absorb her very essence.

The assault of the intercom broke the force binding them together. Kelly moved swiftly to the door of the train. Shane sucked in air between his clenched teeth and watched her leave. *If I concentrate hard enough I can ignore that damn pain in my chest.*

Moments later, he saw her in a window. Tears streamed down her flushed face.

The pain in his chest grew to explosive proportions and robbed him of breath. *You can do so much better than me.* He smiled up at her and waved.

Chapter Two

Everyone steered clear of him after Kelly left. With Christmas just around the corner, festivities and goodwill surrounded him. A black cloud seemed to follow him around, befitting his growly disposition. Shane hadn't heard a word from Kelly since he drove her to the station.

About a week before Christmas, Barry stopped by the shop.

He pulled up a stool next to Shane's. "So how do you really feel about Rita's sister?" he asked.

Without looking up, Shane shrugged his shoulders. "She's okay—for a broad."

"You got to do me a favor." Barry laid his thickly muscled arm across Shane's back. "Kelly is coming home for Christmas. If you're not interested in a relationship with her, then you need tell her. She's a good kid and doesn't deserve to be treated like a piece of yesterday's trash."

Shane looked over at his long time friend and realized that he spoke in all seriousness. He never intended to make Kelly feel like trash. He nodded his head. "I'll pick her up from the station."

Barry patted him on the back as he stood. "Thanks, bro."

"No problem. I really didn't mean to treat her like that, man. She just gets under my skin." A shudder rippled over Shane's body. "I mean that in a good way."

"Unless you want to spend the rest of your life alone, you're going to have to put yourself out there on the market."

"Truth? It scares the living crap out of me."

Barry chuckled. "There are some things in life that aren't worth fighting. I can think of worse things than having my woman next to me in my bed." He winked and left Shane with his thoughts.

After their conversation Shane walked home and showered. Kelly's train came in that afternoon. Barry promised not to tell Kelly who was picking her up. Shane wanted to see her reaction when she realized he was waiting for her.

He sat in the parking lot and chewed at his nails. *You're a damn fool for letting her get to you the way she does.* The door to the station opened. He saw her struggling with her bags to get through the exit. The moment he laid eyes on her, all of his simmering anger dissipated. He jumped out of the truck and jogged over to help her with her luggage.

The sparkle in her baby blues told him all he needed to know.

"Going my way, lady?" he smiled, taking the heaviest bag from her.

Kelly laughed, linking her arm around his back for the walk to the truck.

Shane threw her huge tote in the back and climbed in behind the wheel. He sat for a few minutes, staring at her just standing there by the passenger door before it dawned on him what she was waiting on. *She's waiting for me to open her door. I've never opened a door for any chick in my life.* Shane laughed while climbing back out. He walked over, and with a grand bow, he threw open the passenger door and helped her into the truck.

She giggled like a young girl, and Shane's heart sang with happiness.

* * *

Looking back, Shane hadn't stood a snowball's chance in Hell of escaping. He'd been hooked from the first moment he'd seen her. Shane often wondered if it hadn't been a cleverly orchestrated plan from the start. On Christmas Eve, they mysteriously had the house to themselves. They sat snuggled up on the couch, enjoying mugs filled with hot apple cider.

Kelly turned to him and smiled sweetly. "Would you like your Christmas present right now?" she asked.

Her voice, decidedly sexy, sent a shiver up his spine. "If it makes you happy, sure," he replied.

"Trust me, I won't be the only happy person in the room." She winked playfully before she half skipped, half walked into the next room only to return completely naked except for a large red bow tied across her firm round breasts.

Shane's breath caught in his throat. His groin instantly tightened. She wore a smile that was anything but angelic; the devilish glint in her eye unveiled her seductive intentions. He placed his shaking hands on her shoulders and pulled her to him. He captured her mouth in a long drugging kiss, suckling her full, lush lips. Shane lost himself in the sweet warmth emanating from her exquisite body. In an erotic frenzy, she stripped him of his clothes.

In one swift motion, he lifted her into his arms; his tattoos a stark contrast against her silky nakedness. Shane stared into the depths of her captivating blue eyes. She stared back boldly. A growl erupted from deep within his chest and he wet one of Kelly's lush, rosy nipples with a flick of his tongue before taking it between his teeth and tugging gently.

Kelly arched towards his exploring tongue while Shane moved towards the bedroom with her. He laid her down on the center of the bed and stood back, drinking in her ambrosial splendor.

"Please, Shane." Kelly reached out, begging him to join his body with hers.

Her words shot waves of tingling expectation throughout his rigid body.

Without another word, he lowered himself and reveled in the musky scent of her arousal.

Hours later, completely sated, they lay in one another's arms.

Kelly nuzzled up to his ear. "I'm going to marry you," she whispered softly.

Shane's heart skipped a beat. He knew he'd fallen under her spell. For the first time in his life, he didn't feel like running. Looking down at her sweet face, Shane realized he was exactly where he wanted to be.

On New Year's Eve, a preacher married them at the club. It was a new year and a new life. Shane wore his usual biker attire, and Kelly wore a long flowing dress of pale brown deerskin. Rita and Barry stood by their sides surrounded by a few close friends. They stayed together at the house until spring. Once warm weather arrived, they found a small two-bedroom bungalow perched high in the mountains with a breathtaking view of the ocean.

On their tenth anniversary, Shane presented her with her very own bike: an 883 Ironhead, the perfect bike for a woman with her tiny build. He'd been blown away by her reaction. She'd always professed to be content on the back of his bike but the realization that he wanted to share the road with her brought her to tears.

He borrowed a buddy's dirt bike and took her out each day. She caught on quickly, and in no time at all, suited up for her first ride on the open highway. So she had a chance to get comfortable on her new ride, they took their time the first day. Shane saw the deep concentration etched in the small creases lining her forehead. She'd never looked so beautiful.

Shane took her out every day, and by the end of the month, she ventured off on her own. One day, she returned home bubbling with excitement.

"I just saw a flyer for a Toy Run in Langley!" she sputtered. "Can we please go Shane? Please?"

"Riding in a pack is a whole other ball of wax," Shane replied, shaking his head. Seeing her bottom lip begin to quiver, he knew he'd already lost. With a sigh, he added, "If you're certain you're ready."

The words had barely left his mouth before she jumped up and wrapped her legs around his waist. Shane laughed, trying to maintain his balance as she smothered him with kisses.

The mere scent of her made him tingle in anticipation. After all these years, it blew his mind how this woman still brought him to his knees. He buried his face in her mass of golden curls and nuzzled her neck, inhaling deeply. The musky perfume of her body caressed his senses; he moaned deep in his throat.

Nibbling his way up the pulse of her neck to her delicate ear, he whispered hoarsely, "I could devour every delicious inch of you right now."

She leaned back, clasped her hands behind his neck, and looked him straight in the eye. "What's stopping you?" she teased huskily, licking her lips.

"Oh God, Kelly," growled Shane, crushing her lips with his own. He carried her off to the bed they'd shared for more than ten years.

* * *

The weather gods smiled down on them the day of the Toy Run. Spring flaunted her magnificent splendor, evident in nature breaking open in a kaleidoscope of color from the plentiful Lupins littering Cape Breton's highlands to the fields of wildflowers, bursting in riots of purples, pinks and blues. Through the open kitchen window, they heard the enchanting melody of the magnificent fin whale sounding out its welcome of spring.

Kelly bought two large teddy bears and painstakingly hand-stitched little leather outfits for them. She woke up at the crack of dawn, making sure Shane's black Shovel and her midnight blue Ironhead sparkled before she had him bungee a bear to each of their handlebars. Kelly wanted everything to be perfect on her maiden voyage, coercing Shane into oiling down their leathers the night before.

Her enthusiasm was contagious. Shane took things a step further by buying her a little angel on a bike to pin to her vest. Pinning it on, he told her, "Never ride faster than your angels can fly." She must've commented on the pin a hundred times. Kelly found excitement in the smallest things, one of many endearing traits he loved about his wife.

That day, bikes of every make and model filled the mall parking lot in Langley, where the charity run began. Kelly followed Shane at close range. He made sure to park off to one side so she didn't have to do any fancy maneuvering between the rows of chrome and iron. She barely had her bike on its stand before friends swarmed to congratulate her on her first run. With pride, Shane watched his wife sit on her bike and soak in all the well wishes and compliments.

With over a hundred bikes in attendance, the run went off without incident. Toys of every color and description rolled through Langley. Hordes of well-wishers lined the streets to cheer on the parade of bikers whose intentions were to ensure no child went without a toy at Christmas. At the end of the run, their success was evident in the massive trailer sitting at the edge of the parking lot—a mountain of toys spilled over the sides, a symbol of genuine caring and compassion.

Shane and Kelly headed over to the Clubhouse for an impromptu meet and greet. Kelly's ear-to-ear grin told how pleased she was with herself. She'd kept the pace set with confidence, never once veering from the pack. Shane had never been prouder of his wife, happy to stand back and watch her take center stage amongst their friends. He noticed the sun beginning to set behind the mountains and walked over to where Kelly stood talking with her sister, Rita.

"We better get moving kiddo," he said. "The roads are tricky enough during the day."

"Okay, babe." She beamed at him. "Just give me a sec to say my good-byes."

"She did well today, eh Shane?" asked Rita. With red hair and freckles, she looked nothing like her sister, but she was just as classy as Kelly.

"You bet, Rita." Shane winked, placing a hand on her shoulder. "She had an excellent teacher."

Rita laughed, playfully punching him on the arm. "Just 'cause I love ya doesn't change the fact that you're still an asshole."

"Why thank you. That's the nicest thing anyone's said to me in awhile." Shane sniffed and pretended to wipe a tear from his eye.

Kelly walked behind him and wrapped her arms around his waist.

"Guess who?" She giggled.

"Hmmm, not sure, but if we leave quickly, my wife will never know," Shane teased.

"Yup, you're an asshole!" Rita said.

The three chuckled and hugged good-bye.

Out front of the club, they zipped up their leather coats and pulled on their gloves. Shane kicked his bike to life and called to Kelly, "You be careful. The sun's going down and these roads can get pretty tricky at night."

Kelly gave the thumbs up and started her bike.

* * *

A light drizzle fell from a dreary, overcast sky befitting the somber medley of bikes following the hearse to the graveside. Earlier, more than a hundred bikes had filled the church parking lot. The simple service consoled all those whose lives she had touched.

Shane stood off by himself, an aura about him warding off anyone who dared to come too close. His friends respected his grief process and maintained their distance. They all understood the kind of love they had shared. His close friends knew how difficult it was for him to take the leap of faith in the beginning and lay witness to how it paid off in spades over the years—giving him more happiness than he'd ever believed possible.

Shane knew his friends and family were all in pain too, yet he couldn't bring himself to approach any of them. What could he say? No word in the English language justified why any of this had happened. The one and only woman, or person for that matter, he'd trusted enough to let inside his heart had died—unjustly at that. The driver of the truck would have done him a favor if he'd hit him too.

Shane followed the long, black hearse. Behind him, a procession of bikes two wide followed. Traffic stopped, and storeowners stood on the sidewalk with hands over their hearts watching them pass through the sleepy hollow of Brisdon on their way to the cemetery.

After a short graveside ceremony, every rider tossed a red rose into Kelly's grave. Shane watched the last rider look down at the rose covered casket—a symbol of their love and respect. Shane knew Kelly would be very touched by the gesture and never more proud to be a biker.

Kneeling beside her headstone, he noticed someone standing on the grassy knoll beyond the graveyard. He squinted trying to discern who it was and wondered why the man looked familiar. Unease slithered through him, and he realized the guy had been the biker at the scene of Kelly's accident who had fastened the bell to his bike. He looked around the crowd of mourners to see if anyone else had noticed the man. Everyone seemed absorbed in their grief or had wandered back to their bikes and vehicles. His gaze returned to the knoll, but the strange biker was gone.

Shane shook his head, wondering if he'd gone mad. He looked down into the place where his wife lay. *What am I supposed to do now?* He reached over and laid his face against the cool marble, and whispered good-bye to the only person who had ever *really* known him.

Rita broke free from her husband's hold and ran toward the gravesite, crying hysterically. She flung herself into Shane's arms and sobbed. Shane shot her husband a pleading look. Barry strode over and pulled his wife against his chest, where she crumpled, still wailing.

Barry looked down into Shane's eyes.

"We're all meeting back at the house. Are you coming?"

Shane dropped his gaze. "I can't do it," he mumbled.

Frustrated, the big man nodded and guided his wife back to the parking lot.

"Move 'em out, people!" shouted Barry.

Without question, everyone left one by one.

In that moment, Shane knew what he must do. It would be impossible for him to live surrounded by constant reminders of her. He needed to leave, and the sooner, the better. Whether he liked it or not, he'd have to go to the house and pack a few things. He'd leave a note for Rita to do what she wanted with the house. He had no use for it anymore.

With great trepidation, Shane headed to the house he'd come to think of as a home. The idea of seeing it again scared the hell out of him. It had been a week since he'd last set foot in it. Rita had stopped by the house and brought him a change of clothes. His palms sweating and heart pounding, he turned into the driveway. The planters Kelly had insisted on purchasing sat by the front door, the flowers wilting in the sun.

Shane got off his bike and unwound the garden hose. He soaked both planters down, thinking how happy Kelly would be when she saw what he'd done. The hose fell to the ground with the realization he'd never see her smile again, nevermind hear her voice. *You have to go in there! Suck it up and get it done, man!*

Shane moved decisively to the front porch and turned his key in the lock. He took a deep breath and pushed his way inside. Everywhere he looked, a memory of Kelly flashed in his mind. Her laughter echoed through the house, the volume increasing with each moment that passed.

His hands flew up and covered his ears. Through a steady stream of tears, he stumbled toward their bedroom. Their unmade bed wrenched his heart as he remembered the reason why the blankets lay in a twisted heap.

Shane shuddered, forcing his thoughts to the task at hand. He filled his arms with a medley of clothes and ran from the room. Before leaving, he stopped briefly in the bathroom and gathered a few things. Her housecoat hung from a hook on the back of the door. His trembling hands reverently held the fabric up to his face. He almost choked on her unforgettable scent. He closed his eyes and breathed deeply, branding the smell to his memory.

"Oh God," he cried and bolted from the house for the last time. Shane filled his saddlebags with his things and ran back up to the house and dropped his key in the mailbox. He'd call Rita from the road; he knew he'd never be able to live in this house again.

With a heavy heart he climbed on Belle and brought her to life. Before he pulled out onto the road, he took one last look back at the house he'd shared with the one true love of his life. Life would never be the same without her, and the only way he knew how to heal his broken heart lay in the wind.

Chapter Three

The highway yawned ahead of him, a different breathtaking view around each bend. Kelly would have wanted him to spend their savings this way. If he had to, he'd resort to wrenching bikes for some fast cash along the way.

Over the course of the next few days, Shane fell into a comfortable rhythm. He rode all day, stopping for gas here and there. After a day of hard riding, he'd find a secluded spot to rest. On warm nights, he'd stretch out the sleeping bag beside the bike and sleep, and on cooler nights, he'd build a small fire and curl up beside it.

Shane found a beautiful spot on the fifth night next to a small waterfall. The grassy patch would be the perfect place for a small fire and some sleep. Mentally, he thanked Rita a million times for slipping in a few things he hadn't thought to ask for, like a bar of soap and a towel. The waterfall offered the perfect opportunity for a much needed shower. It didn't take him long to strip down, taking the towel and soap along with his knife just in case he ran into any snakes.

Shane put the towel down at the water's edge and ran in at full speed. The icy water took his breath away and he shot up like a torpedo with a huge splash. Wading in toward the waterfall, he sighed gratefully, the water growing warmer. He climbed up the side of the incline to a platform where the water fell over it.

Standing under the falling water, he thought how easy it would be to jump down into the swirling pools where rocks jutted out precariously. *It can't hurt any worse than the pain I'm feeling now.*

Too bad he didn't have the nerve to take his own life. He had nothing to live for and no reason to die. Kelly wouldn't want that; he knew this for sure. Shane lost the last thread of his composure. He cried and screamed obscenities to the night and the sound of rushing water, shaking his fists at the sky. He hated the man in the log truck and hated himself even more.

By the time he left the water, the sun had just begun its descent. Quickly, he dressed and started searching for firewood. Earlier, he'd spotted a bottle of shine in the bottom of his saddlebag. A note taped to it from Barry that read: temporary fix for a broken heart. For the first time in his life, he understood why people turned to booze in times of heartache. Maybe if he drank himself to sleep he wouldn't wake up imagining he heard Kelly calling out his name. Long as he lived, he'd never forget the sickening crunch of her body hitting the asphalt and breaking every tiny bone in her body.

Shane shuddered at the memory. Within minutes he had a fire crackling through the kindling he'd gathered and began adding larger pieces to the hungry flames. In no time at all he'd built a nice little fire. He made himself comfortable on his sleeping bag before twisting off the cap on the big bottle. Barry obviously thought he'd need a stiff drink. At least out here he couldn't hurt anyone except for himself.

The clear liquid burned down the back of his throat. He gasped, trying to catch his breath. By the time it exploded in his belly, the numbing effects began to travel across his chest. Shane tossed back a healthy swallow from the bottle. Some time later, he sat swaying from side to side, mumbling to the star filled sky.

He tilted his head to the side, hearing the familiar rumble of a motorcycle in the distance. The sound grew nearer, and finally, the strange biker who had tied the bell to his swing arm and who he'd seen across the cemetery sat across the fire from him.

"Who the fuck are you?" he slurred, trying to focus on his campfire guest.

"My friends call me Sam, I just want to help," Sam answered in a deep voice.

Shane laughed hysterically, falling back on his sleeping bag. Once he regained his composure, he sat up again and stared across the fire at him.

"So what's the deal with the bell?" asked Shane, bringing the bottle to his lips and swallowing deeply. He coughed and sputtered, weaving back and forth.

Sam told Shane there were many tales behind the biker bell. "If a biker loses someone they care about to a bike accident, they tie a brass bell to the swing arm in memory of the brother or sister. It's a small thing, but the real reason lies in that when the bell gets dirty and tarnished the owner of it is reminded of the person the bell represents when he takes the time to polish it. The bell also symbolizes being in the wind."

"Bullshit," growled Shane. "You're just talking bullshit now."

"Maybe so," Sam smiled, "but when you leave tomorrow, I know of a place you should go."

"Oh, you do, do you?" Shane narrowed his eyes. The wide brim of Sam's hat hid most of his face, but he couldn't help but feel a sense of familiarity. "Why the fuck should I listen to you?"

Sam leaned forward and pulled a stick from the fire. Using the charred end he etched a simple map on a flat rock.

"Follow this road and you'll find people who will help you."

Morning light filtered in through the looming evergreens. Shane pulled his leather coat up over his head. The slight movement caused a shooting pain to explode behind his eyelids. He winced, trying to remember how he'd got there and why he felt like a piece of shit. The foul taste that coated the inside of his mouth quickly reminded him what he'd been drinking. Thoroughly pissed off at himself, he grunted aloud, attempting to sit upright. With a hand to his head, he took in his surroundings through narrow slits. Slowly he remembered the fire, the bottle...the biker named Sam. He shook his head, counting the times he'd seen the biker. Why was this guy following him? Or was he? It certainly seemed like it, but it could be coincidence...couldn't it?

He stood up and looked around. His gaze fell on the bottle of shine leaning against his front tire. His brow knit, noticing the crude marks on a rock. Bits and pieces came filtering back to him. Where did he give him directions to? More importantly, why?

For the life of him, Shane couldn't remember why. No wonder he never drank. How guys drank that shit on a daily basis was beyond him. It took him a week or better to recover every time he so much as sniffed a cap. So much for it making him feel better. He stretched, but quickly grabbed his lower back. Getting old sucked. He was definitely too old to be sleeping on a pile of rocks.

Shane's belly growled. How long had it been since he'd had a meal? One day? Two? If memory served, there should be a little diner just up around the next bend. He needed coffee and lots of it. Slowly and carefully, he gathered his things together and packed his saddlebags. He tied the sleeping bag to the bars and cleaned his sunglasses with the corner of his denim shirt. The bright morning sun seared his eyes and heightened the pain in his already throbbing head.

Shane breathed a sigh of relief upon seeing the handmade sign for the diner. As he parked his bike, he noted that only one other motorcycle sat in the lot. Shane painfully dismounted and stopped to take a look at the Heritage soft tail. He whistled long and low at the miles of chrome that wrapped from fender to fender.

Maybe it wouldn't be so bad sharing a coffee with a fellow biker, especially one that didn't know about the accident. Maybe for a little while he could escape and be someone else. Shane turned and strode over to the door, opening it with a loud creak that pierced his skull. He grimaced and entered the diner.

"Take a load off," invited the biker. He kicked a chair out from under the table with a well-worn boot.

"Thanks," said Shane and sat down heavily in the chair. He pulled his hair back with one hand and removed his glasses with the other. He squinted against the light filtering in the through grimy windows.

"The name's Zach." He extended a tattooed hand.

Shane shook his hand and introduced himself, looking around the room for a waitress.

"Hey, Louie. We need some service out here!"

Shane held his head in his hands at the sudden outburst.

"Whoops! Sorry buddy," he chuckled sympathetically. "It looks like someone had a few too many last night."

A short man wearing a filthy apron scurried from the back with a steaming carafe of coffee. He took two mugs from under his arm and placed them on the table, filled the cups and produced creamers from the crusty apron's pocket.

"Breakfast okay for you two?" he asked in a raspy voice. Yellow teeth and the unmistakable stench of cigarette smoke set Shane's stomach in motion.

Both men nodded and the spindly man scooted back to fill their orders. Shane picked up his mug, bringing it to his lips. Intense warmth emanated from the cup, and he blew on the rim before cautiously sipping. If God made anything better, he kept it for himself. He welcomed the roasted nectar, the warmth soothing his raw throat.

"Let me guess, you were into the shine?"

"Lucky guess." Shane grimaced at his breakfast companion. "How'd you know?"

"Cause it's coming out of your pores!" he laughed, moving his chair back an inch and fanning the air in front of him.

"Sorry 'bout your luck," growled Shane and sipped from his mug again.

"Whoa there big guy. I'm just having a little fun." He smirked. "I got some aspirin out on the bike. Can I get you a couple?"

"I'll take whatever you got." He yawned, looking through one eye as Zach left the table and walked out to his bike.

Shane watched through the window. Zach stopped, giving his Shovel the once over, reaching over to jiggle the bell. Vaguely reminding him of the conversation he had with the biker. He'd be damned if he could remember the story. *Maybe this guy knows what the deal is about the friggin' bell? Won't hurt to ask.* He finished the last of his coffee and banged his mug on the table a couple of times in an attempt to get the old man's attention.

The door creaked open, and Zach tossed the bottle of aspirin at Shane.

"Hey, Louie!"

The little guy rushed out with the coffee pot in one hand, balancing two plates in the other. Once he'd set their breakfast on the table, he refilled their cups and disappeared into the back of the cafe again. Shane's belly rebelled against the aroma of bacon and eggs. He pushed the plate away and grabbed his coffee mug.

"You okay?" Zach asked between mouthfuls of greasy eggs and bacon, the egg yolk dripping from his sand colored mustache.

"Just swell." Shane held his stomach and turned his chair to face the window. If his new friend didn't stop slurping his food, he'd end up spewing his coffee all over the floor.

It seemed like an eternity before the guy stopped eating, and the little man appeared to clear their dishes. He glanced at Shane's uneaten breakfast and looked pointedly at him.

The biker snorted in amusement. "Shine victim."

The café owner chuckled and walked away with the dishes.

Over coffee, the two discussed the miles of roads in the area that seemed to stretch on endlessly. Roads turned to bike talk as it usually did between two seasoned riders. Before long the topic of the bell came up again.

"It was a gift," said Shane rubbing his jaw. "I might have been a bit shit-faced and be damned if I can remember how the story went."

"Well I've heard a couple stories but the one that has always stuck with me was the one my own Dad told me when I was a kid."

Shane pictured the fat blue fender as he watched his own father drive away all those years ago. He leaned back in his chair and made a concerted effort to listen to Zach's bell story.

"Many Christmases ago, a crusty old biker headed home from a trip to Mexico. His saddlebags were filled with toys for the kids at a group home near where he lived with his ol' lady who understood his need to roam the highways.

"North of the border lurked a small group of little critters known as road gremlins. The gremlins were notorious for leaving little obstacles like a shoe, boards, and pieces of old tires on the road. They were also the cause of those dreaded potholes for bikers to run over and crash.

"Rounding a curve, the gremlins ambushed him, causing him to wreck and skid before coming to a stop next to one of his saddlebags that had broken free. Well, this biker, not being one to give up, started throwing things at the gremlins as they approached him. Finally, with nothing else to throw but a bell, he started ringing it in hopes of scaring them off.

"About half a mile away, camped in the desert, two bikers were sitting around the campfire talking about their day's ride.

"In the stillness of the night air, they heard what sounded like church bells ringing. Upon investigating, they found the old biker lying along the roadside with the gremlins closing in on him. Needless to say, being part of the biker brotherhood, they warded off the gremlins until the last one ran off into the night.

"Feeling grateful, the old road dog offered to pay them for their help, but as all true bikers do, they refused payment. The old biker couldn't let a good deed go unnoticed, so he cut two pieces of leather from his saddlebag tassels and tied a bell to each one. He then tied them on each of the bikes' swing arms. He told the two fellow bikers that if they ever crossed paths with the evil road gremlins, they only needed to ring the bell and a brother would come to their aid."

Zach chugged down the rest of his coffee. His mug hitting the table with a bang and laughed. "My dad always ended the story the same way saying, 'So, whenever you see a biker with a bell, you know he's been blessed with the most important thing in life—friendship from a fellow biker' and he really believed in it too." He laughed heartily and whacked the tabletop again. "Louie! The little fucker is deaf as a doorknob. Not sure why I keep coming back here." Zach stood up, his presence filling the small room.

Just how many stories are there about the stupid bell? Now he wished he had paid attention when he heard mention of them over the years. He'd just assumed it was another useless decoration so many riders felt the need to have.

"Keep the shiny side up, brother," said Shane and held his hand out.

"Back atcha, big guy," Zach shook his hand biker style by linking thumbs, patting him on the shoulder. He tossed a couple bills on the table and tapped his forehead with his fingers in a salute before he left.

Shane got up and found the restroom. He splashed cold water on his face and down his neck before heading out to his bike. Reaching the exit, Louie stood with a bag in his hand for Shane. "What's this?"

Louie just smiled broadly, pushing the bag at him until he took hold.

Outside, he opened the bag and saw a bottle of water and four slices of dry toast. He may have been a strange little man, but he was mighty perceptive in knowing exactly what he needed. Maybe one day their paths would cross and he could return the favor.

Chapter Four

The sun shone bright over Shane's left side mirror. The warmth made up for the brisk ocean breeze. He rode along a straight stretch of road, allowing him to enjoy the spectacular coastal view, complete with wharf after wharf of small wooden fishing boats and paint worn hulls. Shane passed through a number of tiny towns separated by rich farmland and wilderness. The century-old houses nestled in the quaint villages revealed Cape Breton's rich heritage.

The road he traveled began to twist and turn, making it difficult to stay focused after his run-in with a bottle of shine the night before. He'd best pay attention or end up swimming with the whales. Shane looked for someplace to stop and stretch his legs. His body was starting to rebel from riding such a long distance.

As the sun moved closer to the horizon, he started thinking he should find a place to bed down for the night. He smelt the enticing scent of burning pine. A bike turned off the main road up ahead of him, going in the same direction the smell came from. Maybe he'd find some camping bikers to keep him company for a change. Shane still hung a good distance behind the rider. He closed the distance quickly. A lone Evergreen, slightly bowing towards the road, marked the road he'd seen him turn onto. Gearing down as the asphalt turned to gravel, he spotted a village that looked to be settled by Natives. The Micmac tribe still heavily populated Cape Breton, but he'd never seen them living in wigwams like this.

At first the village looked to be deserted. He saw no sign of life from within. A flap opened on one of the larger wigwams and a tall native with snow-white hair stepped out. Shane stayed on his bike, the engine idling while he assessed the situation. If the old guy wasn't happy about him being there, he wanted to be able to make a quick getaway.

The old man looked his way, tilting his head curiously. He walked towards him and raised a hand in a gesture of greeting, which Shane returned, wondering if he spoke English. Feeling nothing threatening in his demeanor, he reached down and turned off his bike.

"Hi there," Shane called out.

"Greetings."

Shane hiked a long leg over his bike and stood by its side. The native had kind eyes and flawless, honeyed skin despite his apparent age. Shane felt at ease in his presence.

"My name is Shane." He closed the gap between them with an outstretched hand.

The old man hesitated, his gaze wandering the length of Shane before accepting his offered hand.

"Welcome." He bowed his head slightly. "My name is Chief Gray Owl and this is my village. How is it you have come to be here?"

"I'm looking for a place to roll out my sleeping bag for the night. I followed the scent of your fire, thinking maybe there was a camp ground up this road."

"I see." He nodded and his gaze wandered over to Shane's bike. His brow arched, and Shane saw a look of appreciation ignite in his deep brown eyes. "What kind of motorcycle do you have here? I have never seen one quite like this."

"This is a 1973, Harley Davidson, Shovelhead. Her name is Belle."

While the two men stood discussing his bike, the tiny village began to stir. A group of women and children laughed and sang as they walked along a path leading into the village. Upon seeing the man with strange markings on his skin, their laughter ceased and they spoke in hushed tones amongst themselves. Most of the children fell back behind the women, peeking out occasionally from behind their long skirts. A few of the men had also made an appearance. Some walked over to their respective mates; others came to the side of their chief.

Chief Gray Owl noticed the unrest amongst his people. He raised one hand before calling out, "My people. I ask you to welcome our guest, Shane."

The village people resumed what they'd been doing. Shane saw that the chief was well respected and studied him curiously. He noticed the wisdom deep within the man's almond-shaped eyes, yet his presence emanated a warm gentleness.

"You are welcome to stay with us this evening," Chief Gray Owl said, interrupting his thoughts. "You must be hungry from your travels. Let my woman prepare you a bowl of venison stew."

"Please don't go to any trouble. I will, however, accept your offer to sleep here tonight."

The chief clapped his hands together, and a native woman dressed in tan deerskin appeared at his side. He spoke in a language Shane had never heard before. The woman nodded her head dutifully and left his side.

"Noni will heat up some stew for you. Come sit with me by the fire and we can talk more about this ironhorse and what causes the deep sorrow I see in your eyes."

Shane didn't know how to respond. Did this chief have some kind of psychic ability that allowed him to read his thoughts? How else would he know the pain he endured? How could he tell this man who opened his village to him he would prefer not talking about it?

Chief Gray Owl led Shane into one of the larger wigwams where a number of native men sat on animal skins around a fire crackling within a circle of stones. Smoke escaped through an opening where long poles met at the top. Small fir branches poked out from under layers of woven reed mats.

Uncomfortable with everyone looking at him, Shane reluctantly sat down next to the chief. Most of them looked on with curiosity, a few glared as if they thought of him as an intruder. Chief Gray Owl began telling the men about his Shovelhead, the tone in his voice showing his obvious infatuation. He talked animatedly, describing the bike's sound as thunder.

Noni entered holding a steaming bowl of fragrant stew. She set it down on the ground in front of him and left without a word.

"Eat, my friend," encouraged the chief. "We all had our fill hours ago."

Shane brought the spoon to his mouth, testing its warmth with his tongue. The delectable aroma filled his senses. His stomach growled, demanding to be fed. Shane polished off the bowl within a couple minutes. It wasn't until he dropped his spoon into the empty bowl that he noticed everyone had stopped talking and sat watching him. He felt his face flush at the realization.

"You have had enough to eat?" Chief Gray Owl grinned.

"Yes, it was very good." Shane patted his belly. "Thank you."

The chief smiled and looked at him seriously. "I see you have a heavy heart. Is there some way I can help?"

The all too familiar ache of his heart intensified hearing the chief speak. He nodded and hung his head.

The chief briefly closed his eyes before he clapped his hands and spoke in his native tongue. Without hesitation, one by one his people stood and left the circle. A couple of men by the doorway briefly assessed Shane one last time before leaving. The flap dropped shut behind them.

"Your heart is heavy—this I know." Chief Gray Owl's voice held a soothing melody. "I can see you are not ready to speak of this and I will not ask you to. I will offer you a place amongst my people until your heart begins to heal."

Shane's eyes dampened at the generous offer. He could think of no reason why he shouldn't accept. He knew he'd have to deal with his loss sooner or later and his friends were too close to be of any help. He simply didn't have the strength to be reminded of Kelly every time he looked in their eyes.

"I see you are a man of pride. If it will make you feel better about staying here, perhaps there is something we can trade."

Shane looked up at the Chief and saw a mischievous glint in his gaze. What did he possibly have with him of any value? "What do I have you would want?"

"You teach me how to ride the ironhorse." Chief Gray Owl grinned.

Shane threw his head back and laughed. "That, my friend, would be my pleasure!"

The chief rose to his feet. "Tonight, we will sit by the big fire."

Shane followed him out of the wigwam. The setting sun cast an orange-pink glow upon the village. A huge fire roared in the center where every man, woman and child sat in attendance. Most of the women wore shawls of lightly tanned deerskin wrapped around their shoulders; they chattered amongst themselves. Their conversation came to a halt upon seeing the chief with the stranger at his side.

Shane sat next to the Chief in the circle. The atmosphere grew silent, all gazes resting on Shane. His tanned skin was pale in comparison to their dark skin. Shadows danced across Shane's heavily tattooed arms, making the images appear alive.

His curiosity far outweighing his fear, a young boy inched cautiously towards Shane and traced the outline of a spider web with his tiny fingers. A native woman came up from behind him and pulled him to his feet. Although Shane didn't understand her words, her tone conveyed her displeasure at his bravery.

What does she think I'm going to do to the kid?

"Maybe I should go," announced Shane. "I'm making everyone uncomfortable."

"Nonsense." The Chief laid a hand on Shane's knee. "It is just that it has been some time since we have had a white man in our camp. Give them a little time to adjust."

"I guess it's a little late to go riding off in search of another place to sleep." Shane frowned in frustration. "I've ridden many miles today. If you don't mind, I'd like to go to sleep."

"Of course." Chief Gray Owl clapped his hands, and within seconds, his wife appeared at his side. He said a few words in his native tongue. "Noni will show you where to sleep. Come morning, we will talk more."

"Fair enough." Shane stood stiffly. "Thank you for everything. I'll see you in the morning."

Noni waited for Shane just outside the circle. She led him back inside the larger wigwam. Shane saw a bed of sorts already made up for him. A number of animal skins lay strewn on the ground by the fire.

"You sleep here," said Noni. She looked at him sweetly. "You will see. Morning sun will bring a new day." Noni left quietly

Shane stifled a yawn. He took off his riding boots and wiggled his toes to coax the circulation back to his feet as he scanned the room.

How cool is this? He clasped his hands behind his head. A smile tugged at the corners of his mouth as he eased into the warmth and softness of the skins he lay on. *I never knew they used birch bark to cover the wigwams. I thought they used animal skins like in the movies.* From what Shane had seen, skins were used in many ways. Most of the clothes appeared to be made from one type of skin or another and some of the natives used them to sit on or as wraps. The large skin covering the entrance looked like moose.

Shane felt like he'd ridden through a time warp to the days of cowboys and Indians. Only now, it was bikers and natives riding black stallions and ironhorses. Shane chuckled to himself.

The wigwam flap opened. Spring's night air brought a chill to Shane. He shivered and pulled a skin up over his shoulders. In the doorway stood an undeniably feminine silhouette. She stepped into the warm glow of the fire. The only time he'd seen a native woman more beautiful was in the movies. It wouldn't surprise him one bit if her name turned out to be Pocahontas.

Her gaze flitted to Shane. She stopped, seemingly startled to find him there. Their gazes locked for the briefest of moments before she looked down to the ground.

"I'm sorry. I did not know you would be sleeping here." She turned to leave, the unique beads strung throughout her chestnut mane clicked together melodically.

"It's okay," answered Shane. "I wasn't sleeping."

The woman stopped and turned just long enough to offer him a slight smile and flutter of long dark lashes. She left, closing the flap behind her. No matter how beautiful he'd thought the native woman was, Kelly filled his mind every time he closed his eyes. *She would have loved it here.*

Chapter Five

Light streamed in through the wigwam's smoke hole. Shane opened his eyes and squinted against the sunlight. He looked around the room and saw he was alone. The fire still burned brightly. At some point during the night, someone must have fed the fire. For the first time since the accident, he'd slept through the night without being rudely awakened by the haunting sound of Kelly screaming out his name.

He shook his head and sat up. From outside, the scent of something delicious wafted inside, tantalizing his senses. He fumbled with his boots, managing with great difficulty to pull them on over his swollen feet. Standing cautiously, his aching body resisted every movement.

I've gotta piss.

He pulled back the flap and shielded his eyes from the brightness outside.

Just outside the doorway, a group of native children sat drawing in the dirt with sticks. Upon seeing him, they ran in a fit of giggles to various hiding spots. Shane chuckled to himself and wondered just how many white men the kids had ever seen. Even if they'd come in contact with only a few, he doubted any of them had looked quite the way he did.

Shane's bladder reminded him it needed relief. He scanned the village looking for an outhouse of some kind. Just past the cluster of wigwams stood a small wood shack in a secluded area.

That must be the john.

He jogged over to it, and just as his hand touched the rope handle, a voice halted him.

"Good morning, Shane." Chief Gray Owl walked up behind him. "The bathroom is over there," he smiled, pointing to a similar hut at the other end of the camp.

Shane nodded and hurried off. Luckily, upon reaching it, the hut stood empty. Slamming the door shut behind him, he heard the Chief laughing in his wake. It seemed like he stood there for an hour as he emptied his bladder. Finally finished, he opened the door to find the chief waiting with a knowing grin.

"Feel better?" he asked.

"Much," said Shane, tucking his shirt into his jeans.

"How about coffee?"

Shane looked at him puzzled. "I didn't think Indians drank coffee?"

The Chief laughed. "This is the twenty-first century! We drink Coca Cola too!"

Iron Horse Rider

Together, the two men walked towards a native woman, who tended to a low burning fire. On top of a grate, a large kettle bubbled with an unknown substance. The aroma emanating from it didn't smell like any coffee Shane had ever smelled. On closer inspection, he realized that laundry filled the kettle. The old woman stirred the large pot with a long thick stick. She looked up at them and smiled a toothless smile.

"Is there any coffee ready?" the Chief asked the old woman.

She nodded and moved to the side of a wigwam. Seconds later, she waddled around the corner with a big steaming pot. The chief hurried to her side and took the pot from her and set it on the iron grate. The woman disappeared inside the wigwam, but reappeared carrying two tin mugs that she filled using a ladle.

"Thank you." Shane smiled at the woman and gratefully accepted the mug. She nodded and turned back to her laundry. He brought the cup to his lips and blew. The smell, rich and full bodied, permeated his senses. Taking a sip, he discovered the flavor heavenly. "Mmm, this is really good."

"It is our own secret blend; I'm glad you like it." Chief Gray Owl motioned for him to follow his lead. He walked Shane over to yet another wigwam where two crudely fashioned chairs sat by its opening. "Sit."

Shane and the chief sat in amiable silence, sipping on their coffees and enjoying the beauty surrounding them. The tree branches bowed with tiny buds on the brink of opening. The children of the village ran in and about the maze of wigwams. The women gathered in various groups, each one tending to a different task. Shane looked around. But where were the men of the village?

"Fishing," said the Chief.

Shane's brow creased and he looked at him with amazement.

"The men," he sipped from his cup, "they are all fishing."

Shane shook his head and smiled. Not only was he looked to for guidance and wisdom by these people, it seemed he read minds as well. *Until I get to know the chief better, I need to be careful what I'm thinking around him.*

Despite the absence of television and the like, these people always looked to be entertained in one way or another. One group of women piqued his interest. Each one had a piece of tree bark rolled on their laps. Shane turned to the chief and opened his mouth.

"They are using the quills to make patterns in the bark. Some will be used to make baskets, and others will make wall hangings to sell at the open market."

"Are those quills from a porcupine?"

"Yes, and they are a bitch to catch!" The chief laughed heartily.

35

Shane laughed too, surprised at the old man's choice of words. "I bet they are."

"I am wondering where it is you come from?" asked Gray Owl.

"I live just outside the small town of St. Mary's," Shane answered. The topic of home darkened his mood.

The chief nodded. "I see the pain in your eyes at the mention of home."

Shane stood up, uncomfortable with the way the subject had turned. "I'm going to check on my bike." He didn't wait for a response, and without looking back, he headed over to where he'd parked his Shovelhead. He ran his hand over the familiar lines of his old friend. Taking a rag from his saddlebag, he checked her oil level. *One thing about the older Harleys, they sure love to spew oil.* Shane noticed she'd already left her mark on the ground beneath her. He took a quart of oil from the saddlebag on the other side and topped her off.

Shane saw the reflection of the chief in the bike's chrome. He stood crouched down with his hands on his knees. Looking askance at him, he chuckled to himself at the look of concentration on the old man's face as he watched him top off the oil.

You, my friend, have got it bad. Shane knew the signs. He stood up and turned to face the chief. "So you want to learn how to ride?" he asked already knowing the answer.

The chief's gray eyes lit up. He nodded and walked over to the bike. "Nothing would please me more."

Shane smiled. "Have you ever been on a bike?"

Chief Gray Owl blushed. "Never."

"How about I take you out for a ride?" suggested Shane. "You wouldn't have a pair of jeans by chance? I'm a little worried about all those fringes on the bike."

Chief looked down at his clothes and back up at Shane. "Yes, I have jeans I use for fishing?"

"Perfect." Shane wiped his hands on a rag. "How about we grab something to eat before heading out, though?"

The two men walked back to Shane's wigwam. The fire out front of it snapped and crackled. With her back facing them, a woman cooked something on an iron grate over the fire. Hearing their footsteps, she turned her head. He recognized the woman from last night—even more beautiful in the daylight.

"Tia, I want you to meet my new friend, Shane."

"Nice to meet you, Tia." Shane smiled and held out his hand.

Tia lowered her eyes, the corners of her mouth lifting slightly. "Nice to meet you also." She turned back to the food she'd been cooking in a large cast-iron pan.

"I will go change," announced the chief. "Tia, bring Shane some coffee. We want to eat before leaving."

"Where are you going?" she asked.

"Shane is taking me for a ride on his ironhorse." The chief beamed at her, turned, and left to change his pants.

Tia scowled at Shane before going to fetch some coffee.

What the hell did I do now? Somehow, he always managed to get himself in trouble. Shane shook his head and sat on a big tree stump. He pulled a long stick from a pile of wood and started poking around in the fire. Whatever she cooked smelled delicious. He saw potatoes in the pan but he wasn't sure about the other ingredients.

Tia seemed to have disappeared into thin air. He wondered if he should stir the food in the pan like she'd been doing. He looked around, and not seeing any sign of her, he stepped over to the pan and poked it with his stick.

"Just what do you think you are doing?"

"I'm just trying to help," replied Shane, backing away from the pan like a child who'd just been scolded.

Tia let out a long breath and grabbed the stick from Shane's hand. Color rose into her cheeks. "What do you find so funny?"

Shane held his hands up in acquiescence. "Nothing," he managed before he burst out laughing.

Tia's doe-like eyes softened. Soon, she began giggling behind one hand. Chief Gray Owl rounded the wigwam, looking at them as if they'd completely lost their minds. Seeing the expression on his face, they lost all resolve.

"What's so funny?"

"I...I'm not quite sure!" Shane tried to catch his breath.

Tia pursed her lips and took the pot she'd been holding, setting it down on the fire. She ducked inside the wigwam. Shane chuckled to himself and sat down on the stump again.

"Tia is my daughter," stated the chief. "Her husband was killed while hunting many moons ago. Soon, her mourning time is over. I have chosen Raven for her to marry."

Shane had heard of such a practice. He had to wonder how Tia felt about it. He knew how he felt and couldn't imagine ever being able to marry again, especially to someone chosen for him.

Tia returned with plates and cups. She poured them both coffee before filling a plate of the potato dish for Shane and her father. She never looked at Shane. Her expression reminded him of Kelly. He'd always known when Kelly was pissed off about something by the way she pursed her lips and avoided eye contact. Shane always knew it was just a matter of time before she'd let him have it. His heart ached with the memory.

Will there ever be a day when it doesn't hurt so damned much?

Shane sighed and dug into his breakfast. It tasted fabulous. He identified the potatoes and some wild mushrooms. The green vegetable he'd never seen or tasted before but it had a tangy nip to it. All in all, an interesting breakfast he thoroughly enjoyed. He felt the chief's gaze on him as he sat waiting anxiously, his leg bouncing up and down with nervous energy. Shane knew waiting to go for a ride was driving the man crazy.

"Are you ready?" Shane grinned knowingly.

Chief Gray Owl jumped to his feet. News spread like wild fire about the chief going for a ride. By the time the two men reached the bike, a group of women and children had formed. One of the older women danced a slow ritualistic dance around Shane's motorcycle. A musky-scented substance burned in a stone bowl that she held in one lined hand. In the other, she held a large feather she used to carry the smoke from one end of the bike to the other. Shane figured it to be a ritual to ensure the chief's safety on the ironhorse.

"I only have one helmet. We should be okay if we stay off the main roads." Shane handed the chief his helmet.

Tia ran toward her father. In her hands, she held an old style beanie helmet.

Where the hell did she find that? He watched her hand the helmet to the chief without a word.

"Thank you." The chief took the helmet and pressed his cheek against hers.

Chapter Six

It was a good thing she'd remembered about the helmet her father kept with his things. She'd be sick with worry if he'd ridden off without one. A mixture of emotions filled her mind. On one hand, she found herself enjoying the company of this tattooed white man. She wasn't, however, too thrilled to have her father out joyriding on this machine he called an ironhorse.

Tia watched the two of them ride out of sight. Now he wanted to learn to ride. The very idea scared her half to death. *What is he thinking? He knows how dangerous motorcycles can be.* Tia turned back towards the fire. *It's going to be a long day waiting for them to come back.*

Luckily, she'd finished all of her morning chores and had a few hours to herself. The water always relaxed her, and if there was ever a time she needed to relax, it was now.

Tia gathered her things to bathe in the ocean. The harsh salt water always dried out her hair. If her father knew she'd brought a bottle of conditioner to their summer camp, he wouldn't be thrilled. She loved most things about setting up camp. Giving up the luxury of hot and cold running water wasn't one of them.

For as far back as she remembered, she'd spent her summers here. Tia understood how important it was to her father that their heritage wasn't lost. During the fishing season, the children of their camp lived the lives of their forefathers, and throughout the long winter months, they attended regular schools and lived with all of the modern conveniences of today's world. In years to come, it was her father's wish that they would teach their children, and so on.

At the bottom of the path, she saw her mother dressing. Mindfully, she quickened her pace until she reached the sandy shore. With the ease of a cat, she snuck up behind her and grabbed her shoulders.

"Ach!"

Tia laughed.

"Tia! You scared the life from me," Noni said with a smile.

"I'm sorry, mother."

"Has your father left with Shane?" Noni's brow creased with worry.

"Yes. I have to say I'm not crazy about the idea." Tia set her bundle down and started unbraiding her hair.

"I knew the moment that ironhorse pulled into our camp that there would be no keeping him away from it." Noni sighed and sat down on the shore. "Come, sit with me for a spell."

Tia took the brush from her hand and sat behind her. "Mother, do you ever get tired of all this?"

"All this?"

"I mean, coming here every summer. I'm not complaining. I just wonder sometimes if there isn't more to life." Tia separated her hair and started brushing one section at a time.

"It is important that we don't forget the ways of our people. How else will our children learn?"

"I know you're right, but doesn't it bother you that the other tribes talk about us?"

"They simply don't understand, Tia. Most of them respect your father and his decision to lead his people the way he does." Noni stood and took the brush from her. "I have a million things to do. Enjoy the water. It is nice and warm this morning."

Tia jumped up and wrapped her arms around her mother. "I love you." The unmistakable scent of vanilla wafted from her hair. "Mother? What soap did you use to wash your hair?"

Noni's eyes sparkled and she reached into the deep pocket of her dress. In her hand she held a bottle of conditioner. "You are not the only one who has secrets." She winked and made her way up the path.

Tia chuckled, stepped out of her clothes, and quickly moved into the warmth of the water. She swam out to a big rock jutting out from the ocean and climbed up on its top. Stretched out, she closed her eyes, reveling in the way the sun kissed her tanned skin.

It wasn't long before her thoughts drifted to the dream she had the night before the stranger appeared in camp. Was it merely a coincidence that Danti came to her then? She'd been slated to marry Raven for some time now. Why would Danti say she'd meet someone worthy of her love? She pictured her husband's kind face looking down at her.

It is time for you to let me go. Open your heart, my love. You will know him when he comes.

* * *

Chief held on to the back of Shane's shirt right up until they made it out to the main road. Once the pavement allowed for a smoother ride, he let go and Shane could feel his body relax behind him. His smile grew wider and wider as the road began to twist and turn. Chief leaned into the turns like he'd been born to ride. Many new passengers had the tendency to tense up and fight leaning with the bike. This made it extremely difficult for the driver to maneuver the bike safely.

The path carved into the side of the mountain offered a spectacular view of the shimmering water below where dolphins frolicked under the morning sun. High in the sky, seagulls soared aloft the gentle ocean breeze. Soon, the wind began to work its magic, allowing Shane a reprieve from his pain. Around every bend, a different experience awaited, all of which were breathtaking.

Shane looked in his mirror. The chief sat with his eyes closed and nostrils flared, both arms extended like wings. *How many times have I done exactly the same thing while riding on my own—with my eyes open, of course.*

The only way to describe the sensation would be to compare it with the gulls gliding through the sky. The average person, who had never experienced a ride on a motorcycle, might never be able to comprehend what drew a rider to the open road. Until they experienced the magic of the wind and the warm sun kissing their skin, it would remain a mystery to them.

Time slipped past. They had been riding a good hour before Shane noticed he needed gas. He remembered a little gas bar not too far up ahead. With a twist of the throttle, he continued up the road. The gas bar looked at least a hundred years old. A lone gas pump sat in front of a tiny diner. Shane hoped it wasn't like one of the many places that sat abandoned throughout the mountains. The summer brought many visitors, but the maritime winters were long and cruel. By late December, some of these roads were virtually closed off. At times like this, the only tracks in the snow were from snowmobiles, snowshoes and wildlife.

Shane eased up next to the gas pump. The chief got off the back just as a weathered old man emerged from inside the diner. He smiled a toothless grin. Chief hurried over to the man and shook his hand.

"Nice day for a ride," said the stranger. He lifted his cap and ran his free hand over a sparse patch of silver hair.

"Can I use your bathroom?" Chief asked, removing his helmet. He pulled out his long braid where he'd tucked it down the back of his shirt.

"Right through that door and to your right." The stranger motioned to the front door before turning his attention to Shane.

"Can you break a twenty?" asked Shane, who just put the cap back on his tank. "If you have coffee, we'll take a couple cups too."

"Come on in! The name's Jimmy."

Shane reached out and shook Jimmy's dirty hand. "Mine's Shane."

Shane wiped his hand on his jeans and followed him inside the dark diner. Jimmy reached around a corner, flicking a switch that brought the room to life. Tables littered the room with rickety, paint-chipped chairs upside down on each. Clearly, he didn't have many people who frequented his diner. Jimmy ambled over to one of the tables closest to them and pulled two chairs down with a puff of dust. He coughed and wheezed, took off his hat, and gave the seats a couple swipes.

"Have a seat. I'll go get those coffees."

Shane nodded and sat down. The musty scent and dust tickled his nose. He pulled a bandana from his back pocket just in time to catch a sneeze. Through watering eyes, he watched the chief enter the cafe. Shane never knew a native could look so pale. Gray Owl visibly paled as he sat in the empty chair. He held his head in his hands and groaned.

"You okay?"

He shook his head slowly. "Be warned. Do not use the bathroom."

Laughter burst from Shane. Considering the shape of the diner, he could well imagine the bathroom's state of cleanliness. Although he had to take a piss too, he opted to wait until they went back outside and he would sneak around back. Jimmy scurried from behind the counter with two cups in his hands. He set them down on the table, and Shane and Chief looked at one another in disgust. The cups looked like they hadn't been washed in ages.

The Chief pushed the cup away and stood. He weaved a little before heading for the door. "I'll be waiting outside."

With a sympathetic smile, Shane brought the coffee up to his mouth, but thought twice before he took a sip. He set the cup down and pulled a twenty from his pocket, handing it to Jimmy. "I think my friend wants to leave. Maybe another time."

Shane didn't even wait for change. Outside, off to one side in the grass, Gray Owl sat cross-legged, his chin resting on his chest; he inhaled deeply and exhaled nice and slow.

Poor guy. I'd better get him back home before they send out a search party.

"Ready to blow this pop stand?" Shane shouted over to him.

The chief looked up, color slowly returning to his face. He smiled gratefully and hurried to the bike. Shane kicked the bike to life and straddled her. His butt had barely hit the seat before the Chief climbed on the back.

Shane chuckled as he pulled out of the small lot and turned back the way they had come. He kept an eye in his mirror. It wasn't long before the chief returned to normal and sported a huge grin.

A hawk swooped down on the road in front of them, snatching up a small rodent of some kind in his talons. Upon a closer view, its wingspan

was twice the size it had looked from above. The hawk flapped once and soared up into the trees with its prize.
　What a magnificent creature.

Chapter Seven

By the time they made it back, the sun shone high in the sky. Women scurried about preparing what looked to be enough food for five times the number of people who lived in the settlement. A group of women and children sat in a tight circle, running bright red and yellow beads in each other's hair. Everyone had changed clothes since they'd been gone. The women wore long flowing dresses of blues, reds and yellows and edged in intricate embellishment of ribbons. Beads hung from the hems of their sleeves and the bottoms of their skirts looked lovely and festive.

"Tonight we celebrate solstice," the chief spoke from behind him. "We welcome the sun back from its journey around the earth. We must call upon Glooscap so the moose roaming the highlands remain plentiful and our nets are always full."

Shane's brow creased. *Who the hell is Glooscap?*

"Come with me. I have something for you to wear to the celebration."

Shane frowned. *No way am I wearing one of those fringed get-ups.* He shrugged and followed his friend. *I guess it can't hurt to take a look.*

Chief Gray Owl disappeared inside a wigwam. Moments later, he came out carrying a black shirt made of soft deerskin. He held it up to Shane. Different sections hand sewn together crossed the chest in red and yellow. He had to admit it really was nice. Not what he'd wear on a daily basis, but it wasn't as bad as he thought it would be.

"It looks like a perfect fit," he announced, looking quite pleased.

Shane sighed and took the shirt. *Like I can say no now!*

"I must ready myself for our guests."

Chief left Shane standing there holding the shirt and hurried back inside his wigwam. Shane sighed, realizing he'd been doing a lot of that lately. He wandered back to his own wigwam to change. Tia stood at the fire cooking again. Shane braced himself for the onslaught. He tiptoed past her, glancing cautiously over his shoulder and slipped inside the wigwam. She wore a look of exasperated amusement on her face.

Shane stripped his shirt off and threw it on the animal skin that made up his bed. The fire burnt low accentuating the deep ripples of his torso that Kelly had always loved. She would lay by his side until she fell asleep tracing her delicate fingers down each ripple. He felt his throat constrict and he choked on the memory. His eyes burned behind their closed lids. Frantically, he tried to form an image of her in his mind.

A gentle breeze blew across his bare chest, and he sensed another presence in the room. He cleared his throat and inhaled deeply, rubbing his eyes roughly with the palm of his hand. The doorway stood empty, but he could've sworn he'd felt someone come in. Could it have been Tia? He pulled the soft deerskin shirt over his head and crept over to slowly lift the flap. Tia still stood in the same place. He heard her humming quietly to herself.

He closed the flap and sat down by the fire, burying his face in his hands. *I'm losing my fucking mind.* He tried again to picture Kelly—his pulse beating erratically. *Why can't I see you Kelly? What the hell is wrong with me?*

Something touched his shoulder and he reached up quickly to find nothing. He whirled only to discover he was alone. Tears rolled down his face. *Kelly? Are you here?*

Shane forced his breathing to slow down. He picked up his soiled shirt and rubbed his dampened face. *You're a fucking pussy. Get a hold of yourself, man!* Shane threw back his shoulders and lifted his chin. He walked purposefully from the wigwam.

Tia stopped stirring the pot on the fire and looked at him with a puzzled expression. The longer she studied his face, the more her eyes softened. She walked over to him and took his hand, leading him to the tree stump by the fire and pulling him down to sit. She straightened her skirt and sat next to him, still holding his hand.

"She will always be with you. Just as Danti will always be with me." Tia took Shane's hand and placed it over his heart. "She is here."

Shane searched her almond-shaped eyes. He saw her pain for the loss of her husband too. How could her father make her marry again when she so clearly still loved her husband? An overwhelming sense of sadness for this woman made the backs of his eyelids burn. They shared a common bond: grief. He patted her hand and smiled.

"Thank you," he whispered.

Tia blushed and bowed her head. She stood up and tended to her pot of food on the fire. Shane watched her for a minute. He'd seen her pain, yet in a heartbeat, she'd managed to summon enough courage to carry on. Before he left the camp, he'd have to learn her secret.

"So, tell me. Who is this Glooscap I hear talk of?"

Tia looked up at Shane and smiled. "Glooscap came to my people from a lightening bolt that struck the sand. He brought with him much knowledge of the constellations and the stars. He taught my people how to hunt and fish."

"He is your god?"

Tia nodded. "Glooscap is our teacher. Our protector. He watches us from the great wall of the mountain. If we please him, we will have plenty of food and good health. If we make him angry, there will be much death after the snow falls from the skies and my people will go hungry."

Shane sat mulling over what she'd just told him. It was evident in the reverent way she spoke that this Glooscap was indeed their god. He'd have to remember to be respectful of their beliefs no matter how ridiculous he thought they were.

Well, if nothing else, it'll be an interesting evening.

The visitors started to arrive. Most came by horses. Others arrived in the backs of pickup trucks. Shane looked at the lineup of at least a dozen horses. He thought of the rows of iron that used to park out front of the clubhouse. These people were not so different from the biker community back home. They lived by a code of their own, and from what he'd seen so far there were no games, no facades here. Shane found himself being caught up in the festivities. Food of every kind filled a long table. A massive pot cooking on a fire smelled deliciously familiar. He hoped for more of the scrumptious venison stew.

People were relatively friendly towards him—even more so after the men spotted his *ironhorse*. Shane gave the small group of men a few minutes alone before he wandered over to see what they thought. They were talking animatedly amongst themselves. Seeing Shane closing the distance between them, the group fell quiet.

"Do you want to hear her run?" Shane asked in hopes of breaking the ice.

One by one their curiosity won over and he received a collective nod. Shane took position and kicked her over in one energetic rush. Belle's loud rumble resounded over the camp. A couple of men backed away, only to sport ear-to-ear grins. Children ran from all directions to see where the loud thunder came from. Shane watched the crowd thicken and twisted the throttle for effect. The children laughed and giggled, some pointing with wide eyes and shouting oh's and ah's.

Shane noticed Tia edging closer to the front of the group. He smiled her way and motioned for her to join him. Excitement danced in her eyes as she made her way towards him.

He reached out. "Hop on!"

Tia inched closer.

"Watch your skirt and legs on the pipe," he shouted over the bike's engine.

She hesitated briefly before hiking up her skirt and straddling the back seat.

"Hold on!"

Shane picked up his feet and started moving. He didn't tear off like he usually would have for fear of spooking the horses. They rode in a wide circle around the camp; cheers and whistles followed them. Shane looked in his mirror and saw Tia wearing a bright smile that warmed his heart. If this ride could take away the pain for even a second, he'd be happy.

After they'd made a couple rounds, he pulled back to their starting point. The children seemed to have changed their minds about him; each one held their hands up to be next. He laughed and called over a young boy of no more than twelve. The boy jumped up and down in excitement. He puffed out his scrawny chest and strutted over to Shane.

Shane smiled knowingly and signaled for him to climb on. "Hold on."

The boy squealed in delight, waving a hand in the air. This set the course for the remainder of the day until metal spoons struck the side of pots to signal suppertime. Shane parked the bike and walked over to the huge spread of food. The meal was unlike anything he'd ever experienced before.

Every type of wild animal conceivable had been roasted: squirrels, deer, moose, rabbit and many others. Massive wooden bowls held brightly colored boiled vegetables. Shane wasn't sure what they used for seasoning, but judging by the smell emanating from the fires, he figured they added something to the wood. Half of the table was covered by a large assortment of dried fish, tastier than any Shane had ever eaten. It was topped off by a bright yellow bread that he learned was cornbread.

Everyone laughed and chatted while eating. Shane couldn't believe the amount of food he'd stuffed in his mouth and still didn't feel like he'd explode. If he had to guess, it was because there wasn't any heavily starched food. The dishes were all organic and cooked or smoked to perfection.

Over the course of the evening, Tia became his constant companion. It brought him comfort to share his time with someone who understood his pain. Not everyone seemed happy about their blossoming friendship. A tall, broad-shouldered native sat glaring at him from across the fire. Shane realized the man could be none other than Raven, Tia's intended.

"Should I be worried?" Shane whispered into Tia's ear.

She waved him off, scrunching up her face. "Don't worry, his bark is worse than his bite. For as far back as I can remember, Raven has been somewhat of an outcast amongst my people. He prefers to spend his days alone. We all have learned it's best to leave him be." She stood, dusted off the back of her skirt, and hurried off to join the other women, who had started to put away the left over food. They worked together like a well-oiled clock, and quickly, each woman rejoined the circle.

"What happens now?" he asked Tia once she'd returned.

"My father is well loved for his stories. If we are lucky, he will tell us one of his tales. Later, when the moon rises, we will make offerings to Glooscap and dance."

Shane shot her a horrified look. "You aren't seriously going to make me dance?"

Tia tilted her head back and laughed. Raven's head jerked towards them and glared vehemently at Shane.

"Not you, silly. Our dancers will dance!"

Chief Gray Owl raised one hand. A hush fell over the circle. He stood, opening his arms wide before he began to speak. His rich baritone voice sliced through the brisk evening air.

"Soon after Glooscap left our people, four men agreed to go in search of him. They did not know where to look, but they knew any man who truly wanted to find Glooscap would be shown the way. They began their journey in the spring of one year and were still searching mid summer of the next.

"The four men happened upon a path in the forest. They followed this path until they came to a beautiful river. They climbed a small hill and from the top they looked down and saw smoke rising through the trees. Before long, the men found their way through the trees to a rather impressive wigwam.

"Inside, they found a middle-aged man and a frail older woman. An empty mat told them there was a third person who lived there. They were welcomed to sit by the fire. Not long after, they heard a canoe approaching. Footsteps brought in a rather well dressed man.

"The old woman stood with great difficulty. She brought in four or five beavers and started preparing them to cook. Her hands shook feebly, and before long, the young man took the knife from the old woman's hands and took care of the beavers. Soon after, he set before the hungry men a good portion of the cooked meat.

"The men stayed for seven days, resting after their long journey. Not once did anyone mention the dirty and tattered clothes they wore. One morning the middle-aged man asked the younger man to wash the old woman's face. When he did so, all of her wrinkles disappeared. Her white hair turned to black and shiny and she now wore a beautiful robe.

"The four men were totally amazed. They then knew their young host had supernatural powers. The young man asked his guests if they would join him for a walk. Beauty was everywhere—the air sweet and balmy. Everything suggested good health and happiness.

"Why have you all traveled so far? What are you in search of?" asked the young man.

"We are in search of Glooscap."

"I am Glooscap," he replied. "What can I do for you?"

"I am a wicked man," said one man. "I have an ugly temper. I wish to be calm, meek and holy."

"I am poor," said the second man, "and I find it difficult to make a living. I wish to be rich."

"I am despised by my people," said the third man. "I wish to be loved and respected."

"Very well," said Glooscap. "Your wishes will be granted.

"I wish to live a long time," said the fourth man.

"You have asked a hard thing," he said. "I will see what I can do."

"The next day they went on a walk and came to the top of a rocky, broken hill. At the top he turned to the fourth man and held him around the wrists. He lifted him high in the air and when he brought him back down to the earth, he became a gnarled old cedar tree, ugly limbs growing out all the way to the bottom.

"There, I am not sure how many years. I can assure you that you will live a long life."

"Terrified, the three men looked on thinking of how Glooscap would grant them their wishes. Glooscap calmed their fears and when they got back to his wigwam, he gave them brightly colored new clothes.

"The men were eager to return home but dreaded the long journey ahead of them. Glooscap offered to be their guide. They reached the top of the first mountain and looked out at the mountain where their home lay. All complained how it would take at least seven days to reach home. They pushed on and reached the second mountain in the early afternoon.

"Look around you," directed Glooscap.

"The three men were surprised to see they stood in their country. When they made it home they had to convince their people who they were because nobody recognized them. Finally they told them all of their journey and time with Glooscap. When they finished, they each opened a box that Glooscap instructed them not to open until they were home. Each box contained a powerful ointment that each man rubbed over his body.

"Each of their wishes were granted. The man who had been hated became a beautiful spirit. The man who had been poor became a successful hunter allowing him to provide for his family. The man with the wicked temper became a calm righteous man.

They found Glooscap and he had granted them their wishes."

Finished, Chief Gray Owl bowed his head and sat back down in his place at the head of the circle. A collective murmur of appreciation traveled around the fire for the story just told.

Shane sat in awe of the Chief's story telling. He painted a picture someone could almost close his or her eyes and see. The night had turned into an interesting and enjoyable one. He looked over at Tia's soft beauty, the moonlight illuminating her in a gilded silver light, and smiled.

Chapter Eight

The full moon hovered above them, casting a welcome silvery light. Some of the older native women raised their hands towards the moon and chanted in a language Shane didn't understand. A few of the men had started drumming on handcrafted drums, the patterns gentle, almost hypnotic. Noni handed her husband a long wooden pipe. Next, she removed a stick from the fire and lit the pipe's bowl packed full of herbs.

Shane watched Gray Owl's cheeks sink in as he drew heavily on the pipe stem. Chief looked at Noni and nodded. She dutifully took the pipe and brought it over to Shane. Puzzled, he looked up at her.

"It is tobacco. Chief Gray Owl wants you to share it with him."

Shane shrugged and accepted the pipe. He drew on it, mimicking the Chief's actions. The thick sweetness filled Shane's throat and he coughed and sputtered. The Chief erupted into a fit of laughter, joined by the entire circle. Thoroughly embarrassed, Shane waved away Noni's attempt to get him to take another puff.

"You must," warned Tia. "You do not want to offend my father."

Shane looked at her pleadingly, and she pushed his hand towards the pipe. He sighed and drew gently on it this time. Quickly, the sweetness filled his senses and left him light headed. Noni retrieved the pipe and returned it to her husband. Shane felt the same way he had as a teenager when he'd been coerced into smoking marijuana.

Shane sat back on his elbows and relaxed on the skin underneath him. He took in the scene before him, as if watching the big screen at a drive-in movie. From time to time, the pipe would make its way back to him again. Each time, and without a moment's hesitation, he toked on the long, thin pipe. His body felt light, like he could float. A totally euphoric sensation he could easily get used to.

Chief Gray Owl stood and faced his people. His stature alone commanded attention. Unusually tall for a Native, he stood eye to eye with Shane. He wore a long sleeved black shirt made of deerskin, adorned with intricate embellishment of ribbons, beads and feathers. His hair, beaded with something akin to a shell, hung around his shoulders and glistened like gossamer in the moonlight. A respectful hush fell over the circle, and Chief Gray Owl spoke,

"O Great Spirit, who art before all else and who dwells in every object, in every person, and in every place, we cry unto Thee. We summon Thee from the far places into our present awareness. O Great Spirit of the North, who gives wings to the waters of the air and rolls the thick snowstorm

before Thee, who covers the earth with a sparkling crystal carpet above whose deep tranquility every sound is beautiful. Temper us with strength to withstand the biting blizzards, yet make us thankful for the beauty, which follows and lies deep over the warm Earth in its wake."

Shane snapped his mouth shut. It was like watching a frickin' movie—or a dream. The sounds and colors blended together until he found it difficult to distinguish between dreams and reality.

The chief continued. "*O Great Spirit of the East, the land of the rising Sun, who holds the sun in your right hand...*"

Tia's leg touched Shane's.

If this is a dream, it's the most realistic dream I've ever had. From beyond the circle, he saw the silhouette of someone approaching. His breath caught in his throat. Kelly emerged from the darkness.

"*Not neglect our gifts nor lose in laziness the hopes of each day and the hopes of each year,*" Gray Owl's voice rang out over the camp.

"Kelly?" His body started to tremble and tears sprung to his eyes.

"Yes, I need you to listen, my love. I do not have much time." She cupped his cheek in her hand.

She looked as beautiful as the day he'd first laid eyes on her, her touch like a butterfly's caress.

"*O Great Spirit of the South, whose warm breath of compassion melts the ice that gathers around our hearts, whose fragrance speaks of distant springs and...*"

Blinking, Shane asked, "How can this be?"

"Hush, I have been watching you. You need to remember that our love is eternal. That doesn't mean you can't love again."

Shane opened his mouth to protest, and she silenced him with a finger pressed to his lips.

"*He who is wise tempers justice with mercy, he who is truly brave matches courage with compassion.*"

"Please don't make our life together all about my death. I'm asking you to honor the love we shared by keeping your heart open."

"I can't," he sobbed, her words kneading his heart. An ache more intense than he'd ever experienced settled in the center of his being and overwhelmed his mind.

"You are destined to love again. Don't think you are dishonoring my memory, for I will be celebrating your happiness. I love you, Shane."

"*O Great Spirit of the West, the land of the setting Sun, with your soaring mountains and free, wide rolling prairies, bless us with knowledge of the peace...*"

"Shane?"

Her hand on his shoulder gently stirred him awake. He slowly opened his eyes, trying to focus. The chief still chanted, the crowd of natives watching him with admiration. Shane realized it had all been a dream. An overwhelming sadness filled his heart. Next to him, he saw it was Tia whose hand rested on his shoulder. Concern filled her eyes.

"O Great Spirit of our souls, burning in our heart's yearning and in our innermost aspirations, speak to us now and always so that we may be aware of the greatness and goodness of your gift of life and be worthy of this priceless privilege of living."

Tia handed him a wooden bowl filled with a pungent red liquid. "It's called sassafras. Drink it."

Shane, suddenly very tired, brought the strange liquid to his lips and drank deeply.

Tia tipped the bowl down, motioning for him to pass it on. Shane blushed and handed it to the next person.

Remembering the dream, his heart ached unbearably. He sensed everyone's gazes upon him as he struggled to stand. Blinded by a flood of fresh tears, he turned and ran into the night.

Voices called after him. He continued to run, tripping on the uneven ground and flailing in the darkness. "This is all so messed up! Fucking ghosts and fucking Indians! Now you see her, now you fucking don't!"

Shane tripped, hitting the dirt with a thud. The skin ripped from his knuckles, and he heard his jeans tear.

"Kelly!" He beat his bloodied fists on the ground and sobbed harder. "Kelly!" He slumped to the ground, allowing his grief free reign.

* * *

Shane struggled to open his eyes. He felt like he did the morning after he'd indulged in too much shine. His head pounded and his hands felt like he'd caught them in a meat grinder. He slowly opened his eyes. Through their narrow slits, everything looked fuzzy. After opening and closing his eyes like a camera lens shutter, things began to finally take shape. He looked up at the opening of a wigwam. Smoke curled upwards and escaped through the small vent hole. The smell of something musky filled his senses.

He turned his head slightly and pain shot through his skull. Slowly, he started to remember the night before. An intense ache resumed in his heart.

Kelly, you came to me. Please come back. Even for a moment.

"Shh," Noni cooed. "You must rest." After she finished wrapping his torn and bruised hands, she pressed a cold cloth to his forehead.

"How did I get here?" Shane mumbled.

"You left the fire and ran into the night."

Shane struggled to put together the pieces.

"Chief and a couple men followed you. When they found you...you were not in the best shape."

An image of his fists beating the ground flashed in his mind.

"When they brought you back here, I could not make out what you were saying. I cleaned up your knuckles and spread sarsaparilla on your wounds before I wrapped them in gauze."

Upon hearing about his outburst, embarrassment settled over Shane. He looked up at Noni. The compassion he saw in her eyes urged a lump to form in his throat. How different his life would have been if he'd a mother as kind as Noni. Her features began to fade, and he welcomed the darkness that enveloped him.

The next time Shane opened his eyes he was alone. It no longer felt like his eyelids were made of lead. He looked around groggily, and tried to sit up, putting his weight on his hands. He cried out and fell back down on a thick bed of skins.

Noni returned to his side. She offered him a bowl of tea made from the blue-black berries of the sarsaparilla. "Come, drink." She helped him sit and wrapped her arm behind him. With strength unbefitting her stature, she helped him sit up. Noni put the bowl of tea to his parched lips.

Shane sipped from the bowl. Once he realized how delicious it tasted, he drank greedily.

"Drink slowly," she scolded. "There is plenty."

Shane flashed Noni a grateful look.

After he'd emptied the bowl, she helped him lie down again. She rolled a skin up and put it under his head. "You had us worried," she said, wiping his brow.

"What happened?" Shane croaked, his throat as gritty as sandpaper.

"Hush, plenty of time to talk later. You need your sleep."

Shane eased back into the comfort of the skins and closed his eyes. Gradually, the events of the previous night seeped back into his mind. The more he remembered, the darker his mood became.

Way to go, asshole. You just lost your mind in front of the whole camp.

He shuddered at the memory. His anger slowly dissipated with the vision of Kelly. Whether or not it had all been a dream, he somehow knew now that she'd be fine. It didn't make the pain of losing her any less, but it did make him feel more at peace. She wanted him to move on, to love again.

Can I? Can I allow myself to love again?

Shane smelled the increasingly familiar scent of tobacco. It seemed everyone in camp smoked. Last night, even the women and children had taken turns with the pipes. He looked through narrowed eyes to see Noni sharing a pipe with her husband.

The flap opened and Tia entered carrying a basin and a cloth draped over her arm.

"How is he?" she asked her mother.

"He is sleeping now, but he will be okay. The sarsaparilla will heal his hands, and time will heal his heart." Noni stood and left the wigwam.

Shane was touched by the concern he saw in Tia's eyes. *She really is a beautiful woman.* He watched her set the bowl down, the fabric of her dress pulled taught across firm, round breasts, the tips perfectly outlined. His sleeping member twitched. His gaze wandered the length of her. Shane imagined her body to be as flawless as her complexion. Big brown eyes gave the illusion of innocence. Her gaze came to rest on him, and he squeezed his eyes together, hoping she wouldn't realize he'd been watching her.

"His heart aches for his wife." She sighed and turned to her father. "I know this feeling all too well."

"Yes, you do. You also know that time is a great healer. Look at you, it has been a year and now you will soon marry again."

Tia bowed her head and her shoulders slumped. "I am not marrying because my heart is healed. I am marrying because you say I am ready."

"Now, Tia. Let's not discuss this right now." He frowned.

"Yes, Father." Tia stood. "I'll come back in a little while and see if he is awake."

Shane groaned, not wanting her to leave.

Tia rushed over to the fire and ladled a bowl of tea. "Drink some more tea. It will help."

Awkwardly, he accepted the bowl from her; very aware of the effect she was having on his body. He drank steadily until he'd drained the bowl of its contents. "What is this called anyway?"

"Sarsaparilla. We make the tea from the berries. The leaves and stalk we grind up and use for cuts and burns. It is on your hands."

"Hmm, multipurpose. It tastes pretty good, almost like I've had it before."

"Root beer," Chief stated. "Sarsaparilla is used to make root beer."

Shane arched an eyebrow. "No kidding? It's really good. Thank you, Tia."

Tia brushed off the thanks and smiled broadly.

"I'm sorry, but the tobacco must not have agreed with me, and I...I saw Kelly last night." He choked on her name, but managed to maintain his composure.

"No need to be sorry." She moved next to him and set down the basin; its contents sloshed from side to side. "Mother said you would want to be washed now." Tia reached in the sudsy water and pulled out a cloth. "If you would take off your shirt, I will get started."

"Get started?"

"I will wash you."

Shane cleared his throat loudly. His gaze darted over to the chief, who sat with a silly grin on his face. "I think I can do it myself." His cheeks grew hot.

Tia dropped the cloth back into the bowl. The water splashed up and soaked the front of her dress. Flustered, she looked down at herself and then back at Shane. With a curt nod, she turned and hurried outside.

Chief Gray Owl stifled a chuckle, but with one look at Shane, he burst out laughing.

Shane tried desperately to maintain his anger. At first, he'd been totally taken off guard by Tia's proposition. After she'd left in a huff, he sat for a moment struggling with shock that turned into confusion. Now, watching the chief howling at him, he became pissed. The angrier he became, the more the chief laughed until Shane started chuckling at himself too.

Many minutes passed before the chief sat up, gasping for air and wiping tears from his eyes.

"Would you mind telling me what the hell is so funny?"

"If...if you had seen your face!" Gray Owl gasped. "You looked just like a deer caught in a car's headlights."

A bit embarrassed again, Shane grinned. "Well, it's not every day a guy has a beautiful woman ask to bathe him!"

"She only wanted to wash your face and neck—maybe your back and chest. How do you think you're going to manage with your hands all bandaged up?"

Shane looked down at his hands. His brow arched and he cocked his head to one side. "You're going to help, that's how."

Chief blinked and scrunched up his face. "You can't be serious?"

"I am, and you will." He smirked. "That is, if you still want to learn to ride my bike."

Iron Horse Rider

Shane took great pleasure in watching the chief's eyes narrow into slits. With a heavy sigh, Gray Owl stood, walked over to the bowl, and picked up the cloth.

"If you tell anyone…" The Chief waited for Shane to remove his shirt and proceeded to wash him down quickly and efficiently. Finished, he threw the cloth back in the bowl and returned to his seat. He filled up his pipe from a pouch that hung around his neck and used a stick from the fire to light the bowl.

Chapter Nine

Noni opened the flap a crack and popped her head in. "Dinner is ready. Would you like your dinner brought here?" she asked.

Still a little embarrassed about his outburst, Shane readily accepted the offer. The chief helped Shane to his feet, and with an arm draped across the older man's shoulders, they walked outside to sit by the fire. The sun was just beginning to set behind the mountains.

How long was I out? He guessed at least a day. A quick look around the camp revealed that all of the visitors had left.

Out front of the wigwam, Tia tended to the fire. She didn't look in his direction, but turned to her father. "Supper is over at the main dwelling tonight, Father."

Chief Gray Owl nodded. "You will have supper here with Shane. I have some things I need to do."

Tia opened her mouth and snapped it shut. Muttering under her breath, she stormed off.

"She is a good girl, *most* of the time," said chief. "Soon she will marry Raven and he can keep a reign on her." He walked away and left Shane alone with his thoughts.

After the Chief had gone, Shane sat staring into the fire. His nostrils twitched. The wind carried a most heavenly scent to him. He saw Tia coming towards him balancing two bowls in her hands and a small loaf of homemade bread tucked in the crook of her arm. She gave him his food without looking up and sat on the other side of the fire.

"Tell me something," he said. "What have I done to piss you off?"

Tia looked up from her bowl, her brow creased. With a heavy sigh, she replied, "I am not mad at you. I'm mad because it seems I'm always being told what to do."

Shane couldn't help but chuckle, which seemed to infuriate her all the more. She dropped her spoon in her bowl and stood with hands on her slender hips.

"It is not funny!"

"I'm sorry. I'm not laughing at you." Shane wiped his mouth on his sleeve. "You don't have to stay with me if you don't want to."

Tia's features softened. "I didn't mean to take my frustration out on you." Heaving a sigh, she walked over to the woodpile and picked up a log. Teetering precariously at the edge, she placed the log in the low burning fire. Her long beaded hair hung over one shoulder, allowing Shane a glimpse of her slender neck.

"Truce?" offered Shane, holding his bandaged hand out.

Tia rolled her eyes. The slight lift to the corners of her mouth told all. Shaking her head, she reached over and gently took his hand in hers. "Does your hand hurt?" she asked.

"My pride hurts worse," he confessed.

Tia met his gaze. Shane saw genuine concern in her eyes and it touched his heart. "I hear congratulations are in order?"

Tia looked puzzled. "Congratulations?"

"You're getting married soon, right?"

Her shoulders sagged and her eyes filled with moisture. She sat next to Shane, looking so sad he wanted to scoop her up in his arms and make the pain go away.

"You're not happy about marrying Raven?" Shane hoped the question would offer her the opportunity to talk to him about it. He'd seen her grief and knew this couldn't be easy for her.

"Raven is nothing like my husband. He takes great pleasure in the fact that many fear him. I don't know why he is the way he is. All I do know is that I will never love anyone like I loved my husband, Danti, again." Although she barely spoke above a whisper, Shane still detected a tremble in it.

"I understand. I feel the same way about my wife, Kelly."

Tia looked up at him.

"If you're not ready to marry again, why don't you talk to your father about it?"

Tia smiled wryly and shook her head. "You don't understand our ways. It is most important I marry again. Danti and I had no children. I must have a child before I'm past the birthing age."

Shane had read somewhere how much children were expected and desired in a marriage. Since her marriage ended before any were born, she was obligated to remarry and have a child. It wasn't uncommon for a woman's father to choose a husband for her.

"I really am sorry for your loss, Tia. I know how heavy your heart is. Is there no other way?" His heart ached for this woman he barely knew. "I'm not sure I can help, but I'm a good listener."

Tia looked up at Shane again; tears escaped her doe like eyes. She offered a wan smile. "Thank you. It feels good to talk about this, even though there is nothing that can be done to change things."

Shane reached over and rested his hand on her shoulder. He looked her straight in the eyes and smiled. "I'm happy to be your friend, Tia. Perhaps we can help each other."

Tia nodded and slid over, hugging him quickly. "Thank you."

He looked over her trembling shoulder and saw Raven standing across the way in the shadows. Even from this distance, he saw the fire emanating from the man's jet-black eyes. There was no doubt in Shane's mind that he meant trouble for him.

Maybe half the village is scared of him, but I'm not. Bring it on! You don't scare me...brother.

* * *

Shane lay on his bed of skins and reflected on his discussion with Tia the night before. They talked long into the night while waiting for the Chief to return.

Despite his vow not to let anyone get close to him ever again, it surprised him how much he opened up to Tia. It comforted him to able to share his grief.

He now completely understood how much Tia loved her husband. Forcing her to marry again was wrong on so many levels. Not only was she expected to marry Raven, whom she did not love, but to also have a child with him. How could a father force his daughter to lie down with a man she didn't love? Surely, he wasn't the only available man in camp. It wouldn't surprise him if she turned in to a bitter and angry woman. How sad to be robbed of her sweet and gentle spirit.

Why did the chief choose a man whose personality differed so vastly from Tia's? Spending the rest of her days with a man like him will alter her loving spirit.

It amazed him how much his life changed over the past few weeks. He'd gone from being happily married to the woman of his dreams to living in a wigwam amongst a group of natives he barely knew. He realized it probably wasn't his place, but he had to talk to Chief about this. He'd never be able to live with himself if he didn't at least try.

Shane looked down at his bandaged hands. He wondered just what kind of mess he'd made of them. He slowly curled his fingers up and straightened them out. They felt stiff, but he didn't experience any of the shooting pain he had yesterday. He carefully began unwrapping the gauze.

The flap opened, and the morning sunlight streamed in. Noni entered with a bowl of steaming water. Startled, Shane looked up at her.

"Let me help." Noni put the bowl down beside Shane and knelt. Dried blood stuck the last layer of gauze to his knuckles. She moved his hand over to the wooden bowl and placed it in the warm water and repeated the process on the other hand too.

Shane watched Noni tend to his hands. Her demeanor emanated strength, yet her touch felt so gentle. He wondered how different his life would have been if he'd had a mother like her.

"How bad is it?"

Noni carefully put her hands in the water with his and gently peeled the gauze from his knuckles. "It's good," she replied.

She carefully placed his right hand on her skirt. His knuckles weren't raw and red like he imagined. Instead, they were a healthy pink and had already begun to heal.

"Thank you Noni." Shane held his hand out for inspection. "Whatever you did seems to have worked."

"I give you some cream. Each day you put some on." Noni instructed, patting his other hand dry. "Now you will have no scars."

Shane threaded his fingers with hers. "Thank you," he repeated, looking deeply into her brown eyes.

"It is nothing." She shrugged. "One more thing." Noni walked over to the flap, reached outside, and pulled a small stack of clothes inside. "You put these on. I will wash your dirty clothes."

Shane nodded. He didn't have the heart to tell her he had clean clothes in his saddlebags. He would wear these now and save his other clothes for after he left the camp.

Noni had left him a soft deerskin shirt, pants, and a pair of boxers in the package. *What no loincloth?* He laughed, stepping out of his clothes and slipping into the boxers. He wrung out the cloth still sitting in the soapy water and began to wash himself. *What I wouldn't give for a shower.* Shane pulled on the foreign clothing. He shook his long hair free of its ponytail and finger-combed it. *Yuck!*

Outside, the chief sat smoking his ever-present pipe. Shane grimaced at the smell. "Good morning, Chief."

"Good morning." The smoke curled up around Gray Owl's head and created a halo effect. "It looks like you are feeling better."

"Much better." Shane smiled. The fresh smell of the ocean hung heavily in the air. The urge to be in the wind filled his thoughts. "Nice day for a ride," he said.

A spark of interest ignited in the chief's deep brown eyes.

"What do you think, Chief? Are you ready to learn how to ride?"

Gray Owl smiled broadly. "I can think of nothing that would please me more." Rising to his feet, he added, "But first we must have coffee."

"You read my mind." Shane followed him to Noni's cooking fire. The rich aromatic scent of brewing coffee filled the air. They each sat down with a cup.

"Your daughter is not happy about you learning to ride."

Chief's brow knitted. "Why would she have a problem with it?"

"I think she's scared you'll be hurt."

Chief nodded. "I see." He looked over at his wife, who packed him a fresh pipe. "You will talk to Tia," he told Noni. She nodded and exchanged a peculiar look with her husband.

Shane hoped he didn't get Tia into any trouble by letting the cat out of the bag.

Noni handed Chief his pipe and refilled their cups before she hurried off. Shane noticed the chief had lost his excitement about riding. He sat puffing on his pipe, seemingly lost in his thoughts.

Throughout the community, various activities were underway. Under an enormous willow tree, a dozen or so children sat in a circle. In the center, a woman gestured with her hands.

Shane noted how the children seemed totally entranced. *She must be a teacher, and class is in session.*

The morning sun caught the chrome on Shane's bike. He'd love to just hop on her and go, but he'd promised to teach Chief how to ride and that's exactly what he was going to do.

Chapter Ten

Shane turned to the chief, who still stared off into space. "Well, Chief. Let's get this show on the road."

Gray Owl jumped in his chair. "Yes," he said. "I'm sorry. I must have been someplace else."

"Do you have a pair of boots or hard-soled shoes?"

Chief thought for a moment. "I have work boots. Will those work?"

"Definitely. Why don't you go put them on, and I'll meet you over at my bike?"

Chief smiled and hurried over to his wigwam. Shane emptied his cup and headed over to his bike. He'd barely made it there before he heard a clumping noise behind him. Turning, he saw Chief jogging towards him. With each step, Gray Owl picked his feet up in the air much like a horse trotting. His long hair trailed behind him and he wore a huge grin. Shane stifled a laugh at the image.

"Okay, Chief. First, I'm going to show you where everything is on Belle, so listen up. You're going to show me where everything is after I'm done."

Chief nodded, watching Shane's every move. "See this valve down here?" asked Shane. "It's called a petcock and it turns the gas on."

Chief nodded.

Shane put his hand on the left hand grip. "This is your clutch and it's also down here, plus this is where you shift gears. So far, so good?" he asked, moving to the other side of the bike.

"Yes." Chief followed him, his brow creased, and waited for Shane to continue.

Putting his hand on the right grip, Shane continued: "This is your throttle, and here is your brake." He reached down and folded out the kicker. "This thing is the kicker. Now, see this valve right here? It's the choke. Do you think you can remember all this?"

Chief Gray Owl pursed his lips and scratched the back of his head as he walked around the bike. Quietly, he studied the motorcycle as if slowly absorbing everything that he'd just been told.

"Okay, now you tell me what you've learned." Shane stood back and listened to the chief. Finished, Gray Owl stood shifting from one foot to the other.

"You've done well," Shane praised him. "Okay, now I'm going to show you how to start Belle up. I want you to watch closely because I'll have you do it next."

"Thank you."

Shane chuckled. He couldn't remember if he'd been as excited when he'd gone for his first ride. His situation had been a little different. He'd spent an entire winter building Belle, and knew every bolt and wire before he even started riding her. He straddled his bike. Going through the motions, he explained step by step what he was doing.

He reached down and turned on the petcock and pulled out the choke. He gave the throttle a twist and turned on the ignition. Reaching down, he flicked out the kicker pedal and stood up. Shane put his foot on the kicker pedal, his left hand on the clutch. Holding the throttle, his finger extended to hold in the front brake.

"When you push down on the kicker, you're going to pump it a couple times. You can feel the compression building up. I'm going to kick her over now. Pay attention to how I move my leg out of the way once I kick her over."

Shane brought his weight down on the kicker and the old Shovel roared to life. He feathered the throttle. With his left hand, he held the throttle and reached down with his right hand to gradually push in the choke. Returning his right hand to the throttle, he put the bike in gear with his foot and released the brake.

Leaving the Chief behind, he took a quick scoot around the camp. Even after all these years riding, he still experienced an adrenaline rush riding the old Shovel. Chief Gray Owl stood waiting for Shane to return. A few men had gathered around him. He saw Tia and Noni close the distance between them and the chief. Noni held Tia's hand, and Shane saw the concern etched in her face as he pulled up next to the chief. He put the bike back on its stand and dismounted.

"What do you think, Chief? Think you're ready to give her a go?"

"I would very much like to try."

Shane handed Chief the key. "Give her a go, then. Just take it easy until you get the feel for her. Don't forget to move out of the way of that kicker. Trust me, you don't want to get kicked back or you'll be going for a trip over the handlebars."

"Do you think I can do this?"

"Sure you can." Shane smiled reassuringly. "Just remember what I told you and you'll be fine."

Noni and Tia reached his side. Shane saw fear in Tia's eyes. She trembled, her knuckles white from squeezing her mother's hand.

"He'll be fine, Tia." Shane tried to set her mind at ease.

She forced a slight smile.

"Okay, Chief, go for a ride," he said.

Gray Owl took a deep breath and exhaled slowly. He threw back his shoulders and straddled the bike. Shane watched the chief's every move. He did everything exactly as Shane had shown him. He pumped the kicker three times before coming down hard. The Shovel roared to life. Upon seeing the Chief quickly move his leg back, Shane let out a big breath. He gradually pushed in the choke and let the clutch out. With a twist of the throttle and a huge grin, he popped her into gear and moved forward.

The small crowd that had gathered let out a boisterous whoop. They clapped and laughed while watching their chief ride the ironhorse. Although a little wobbly at first, the second time around had him grinning from ear to ear as he rode smoothly around the camp. Shane watched a smile spread across Tia's face, her gaze trained on her father. He caught her attention and winked, making her blush.

Seemingly out of nowhere, Raven appeared, sliding a possessive arm around her waist and pulling her to his side. Shane watched the sparkle vanish from her eyes and noticed the tense posture of her body. The overwhelming urge to wipe the smug look off of Raven's face suffocated him.

On Gray Owl's third trip around, he let out a celebratory whoop. Finally, he brought the bike back to Shane, looking ten years younger than when he'd left. He pulled to a stop, and Shane watched his eyes grow wide as the bike started leaning over to one side. Luckily, Shane reached him in time to hold the bike upright.

"You might want to put your feet down next time you stop." Shane laughed.

Chief Gray Owl looked stunned. He shifted from shock to embarrassment, and finally, he chuckled at himself. He shut down the bike and slid off.

"I knew it would be incredible, but I had no idea it could be so much more!"

Shane laughed, knowing that now that he'd taken a ride, it wouldn't be his last. He'd bet money the chief would have a bike of his own this summer.

Chief offered his hand to Shane. "How can I thank you?"

Shane shook his hand. "There's no need, my friend. You've opened up your home to me, so that's thanks enough."

"You are welcome here for as long as you wish."

His words touched Shane, but in the same moment, he sensed Raven seething at the Chief's display of gratitude. He certainly wasn't earning any brownie points with the man.

Never one to back down, Shane turned, looking him square in the eye and smiled. He gazed down at Tia's ashen face. "How about I take you for a ride and show you there is nothing to fear?"

Tia's eyes grew wide, and she looked from her father to Raven and back to Shane. With a slight smile, she stepped forward. Raven's hand fell from her waist. The rage brewing in his coal black eyes echoed his disposition.

Shane arched his eyebrows in a subtle challenge for him to try and stop her. *Come on make a move. I dare you.*

Raven held his gaze, the muscles in his neck flexing. Reaching out to Tia, he took her by the hand and gave her a helmet to put on. Shane instructed her to come around to the other side of the bike. He reminded her where to put her foot on the peg and hike herself up on the back.

Tia nodded and dropped her gaze.

Shane straddled the Shovelhead while tightening the strap on his helmet. He looked from Raven's intense scowl to the confused look in the chief's eyes. Behind him Noni stood with her eyes big and her hand covering her mouth.

Shane stood and prepped things to kick the bike over. Tia's mother hurried over and whispered something under the flap of her helmet. She scurried off around the bike to her husband's side just as Shane came down hard on the kicker and it started with a rumble.

Noni jumped a good foot off the ground and shrieked. Her gaze found Shane's, and he winked, sporting a devilish grin. She hid behind her husband. Chief Gray Owl laughed at his wife. Raven exhaled, puffing out his chest and wringing his hands.

"Hop on!" Shane shouted over the noise of the bike. Hiking up her long skirts, Tia displayed sexy, slender legs. *Too bad I'm married.* He closed his eyes and shuddered at himself forgetting he wasn't married. Tia settled in behind him, and he pushed the thought from his mind. "Hang on!"

She wrapped her arms around him and held the sides of his shirt in her fists. Shane looked back to see her wide, bright eyes and her lips planted firmly together.

"Here we go!"

He twisted the throttle, cruising away from the camp. In the mirror, he saw everyone waving except for Raven, who had moved to Gray Owl's side. The expression on his face told Shane he'd have plenty to say to the chief while they were gone.

Chapter Eleven

Shane inhaled deeply, never tiring of the intoxicating scent of nature in full bloom. No matter what was going on in his life, he could always count on one thing: the comfort he found from being in the wind. Nothing calmed his spirit faster than going for a ride. On one side, heavily laden trees lined the road. On the other side, the rocky incline led down to the ocean, its creviced surface littered with blue, pink and red wildflowers. It just didn't get much better than this.

Shane looked back at Tia in the mirror. She smiled broadly, stretching her neck to see the bevy of fishing boats out on the water. He noticed the odd canoe amongst the paint-chipped hulls and wondered if they were from Tia's village.

He hoped Raven wasn't giving the chief too hard of a time. He'd worry about all that when they returned. For now, he'd enjoy the hot sun beating down on his face and the breeze blowing in off the ocean. He willed the wind to take away all thoughts of Raven.

They'd been riding for almost an hour before he noticed Tia starting to squirm behind him. She either needed to use the bathroom or was experiencing her first case of biker butt. Just ahead, he spotted a small gas bar and variety store. He signaled and turned into the small lot, easing up along side the gas pump.

They both climbed off the bike. Tia smoothed her skirt down over her legs. Her cheeks, flushed from the wind, glowed and her eyes sparkled. She removed her helmet, smoothing down a few stray strands of hair and running her fingers down the length of the plait she'd thrown over her shoulder.

"Why don't you go find the bathrooms? We'll grab a cold drink and rest a bit before we go any further."

"I'll be right back," she said before heading over to the front door. Just as she reached for the handle, the door opened from within almost knocking her off balance. She yelped in surprise.

"I'm sorry little lady. Didn't mean to scare ya," apologized a hunchbacked old man.

Tia laughed, her face turning red. "I was just looking for the bathrooms."

"Turn to your right once you get inside." He held the door open for Tia to slip past him into the store. The old-timer closed the door and strode over to Shane. "Good day young fella," he said. "That sure is a nice looking machine you've got there."

Shane held out his free hand. "Thank you. The name's Shane."

"My friends call me Billy. Pleased to meet you." Billy pumped Shane's hand. "Where are you headed?"

"No place in particular." He handed Billy the nozzle and screwed the cap back on his tank. "Do you have anything cold to drink?"

"Yup, come on in and take a look."

They entered the store just as Tia opened the bathroom door. She smiled shyly and hurried over to stand beside Shane. They bought two bottles of water, paid for the gas, and headed outside.

"Let's find a place to sit and enjoy the view." Shane suggested, holding the door open for her.

"That sounds wonderful," she replied.

From behind the cash register, Billy smiled and called out, "By the way, there's a couple of old chairs around back of the store. You're more than welcome to sit for a spell."

"Thanks, Billy," replied Shane.

Around back of the tiny store, they found an alcove of sorts where the grass had been neatly trimmed and two high backed wooden chairs sat facing the panoramic view of the ocean.

"Wow." Shane whistled long and low. *Who'd have thought a little piece of heaven would be back here?*

"It's beautiful," Tia whispered, looking out over the edge of the rocky incline.

"Let's sit a while. You're not in any hurry to go back, are you?"

"What do you think?" She frowned and walked over to one of the rain-worn chairs.

"Sorry, dumb question." He laughed and sat next to her, his gaze moving to the vast ocean. Everything else seemed to pale in comparison to it. "Do you ever wonder what's out there?"

Tia followed his line of vision to the water. "Out where?"

"Beyond this island and these mountains."

Tia closed her eyes briefly and sighed. "What was your wife like?"

Shane's pulse quickened and the back of his eyelids started prickling. He exhaled noisily and smiled. "Kelly was just a little bit of a woman with a heart the size of this ocean. I think you would've liked her."

"You love her very much?"

"Yes, I love her very much. Kelly's gone now, but my love for her is very much alive."

"I know. I love my Danti—very much."

"You weren't married very long before he died, were you?"

"No, but I loved him for as far back as I can remember. Even as a young girl, I'd dream about being his wife and having his child." She sighed, one corner of her mouth lifted slightly with a memory. "We would have created beautiful babies."

In her eyes, Shane saw her love for her husband. She wore the same expression Kelly used to have when they talked about having children.

"Why do you care so much if I marry Raven? You will leave one day and go back to your people." She brushed at tears spilling from her eyes.

"What if there was someone else?"

"I don't understand." Her brow creased.

"What if someone else wanted to marry you?"

"There is not one man amongst my people who would dare defy my father's wishes. Besides, I love my husband. What difference does it make who I marry? Whether it's Raven or someone else, I will not love him."

Tia stood and walked to the edge of the rocky incline. The wind wrapped her long skirt snuggly around her legs

"I think we should go back now." She turned around suddenly. "My father will be worried."

Without so much as a glance in his direction, she hurried off towards the bike. By the time Shane caught up to her, she'd already put on her helmet. He reached for her hand, wanting to explain himself to her. She pulled away, as if his touch scorched her.

"Please, Shane. We must go."

Shane saw she didn't want to discuss it any further. It broke his heart to think how sad she must be. He needed to talk to her father. Perhaps he'd make him see exactly how this whole ordeal affected his daughter. If he didn't at least try, he wouldn't be able to sleep at night.

Shane straddled the old Shovel and kicked her to life. Tia silently slid behind him. She'd shut her emotions down, and he certainly could relate to that. Since Kelly died, he'd become somewhat of an expert on shutting down his feelings. He rode home slow and steady, enjoying the wind gently caressing his face. No other medicine soothed his soul like a ride on a beautiful day. Hopefully, Tia was reaping the benefits of it too.

Shane turned down the road leading to camp. The scrumptious smell of meat roasting on a spit greeted them. Women tended to various fires throughout the camp. A group of men returned from the path that led to their canoes and fishing boats. They carried nets filled with fish between two poles. The smiles and laughter amongst them told Shane they must be pleased with their catch.

A number of children ran towards the sound of the bike. Tia warned them all to stay back from the bike's hot pipes. Shane scanned the camp for the chief or Raven and found no sign of either of them. Perhaps they'd gone fishing and weren't back yet.

Tia put her helmet on the back of the bike and turned to leave, murmuring her thanks for the ride. She hurried over to her mother, who cleaned and hung the fish the men had brought back.

Shane knew she wasn't angry with him. She just didn't want to talk about her inevitable marriage. *I don't blame her.*

He repeated the warning to the children about the hot pipes. He needed to figure out the best way to approach the chief, but he didn't want him to think he was trying to tell him what to do. If he could just get Gray Owl to see how this marriage would hurt his daughter, maybe then he'd reconsider his decision.

"Shane!"

He turned to see Chief Gray Owl calling him over to the larger wigwam. Shane took a deep breath and walked toward him. *No time like the present.* He threw back his shoulders, cleared his throat, and pulled back the flap.

Inside the wigwam, the chief sat alone by the fire smoking his pipe. He looked troubled and motioned for Shane to sit by him. "Come," he said. "We must talk."

Uh oh! I bet Raven has been ragging on the old man the whole time we were gone. Shane sat next to the chief, nervousness settling in his gut.

"What seems to be the problem, Chief?"

"You are very perceptive. Did Tia enjoy her ride?"

"Yes, very much so." Shane drummed his fingers on the ground. *Come on, spit it out.*

"Raven is not happy. He does not think his future bride should be going off on her own with another man."

Shane couldn't help but laugh, but upon noticing the chief's dark expression, his laughter died. "He has nothing to worry about. We are merely friends."

"I know this. I also know that Tia is not happy about marrying Raven. It will be hard for her at first, but she will adjust and make him a good wife and mother to their children."

"What about love?" Shane asked.

Chief chuckled. "Love? In time, they will come to love."

Shane shook his head. "She is still grieving for Danti. If you force her to marry a man like Raven, she will become a bitter woman."

"Why do you care so much if Tia marries Raven?"

"If I thought it would save Tia from a life of sadness, I would marry her myself."

Chief's brow rose and he sucked on his pipe, seeming to ponder his words. "Why would you do this? I know how much your heart aches for your own wife."

"I think it is wrong to make her marry a man she doesn't love. Raven will only bring her sadness. As her father, how can you condemn her to such a life?" Shane regretted his choice of words the second they left his mouth.

"Raven is the eldest man in camp without a wife. It is a woman's place to have a child. Tia is not getting any younger. If she does not marry soon, the other women will cast her out. I am only thinking of her happiness. Contrary to what you think, I love my daughter."

"I'm sorry. I didn't mean to imply you don't love her, but there has to be another way for Tia."

The two men sat in silence. Shane watched the old man chew the end of his pipe, occasionally drawing a puff of smoke.

"I am in need of sarsaparilla. It is found in the highlands."

What the hell does that have to do with anything?

"Come morning, you and Raven will leave for my brother's camp and bring some back to me."

"Pardon my interruption, Chief. Just what exactly does that have to do with Tia?"

Chief held his hand out. "Let me finish."

Shane breathed in deeply and exhaled slowly, trying to calm himself so he could hear the chief out. He nodded.

"You will both leave at the same time. What path you choose is up to you. The one who comes home first will win Tia's hand."

Stunned, Shane's eyes widened and his heart began beating faster. *Win Tia's hand? Marry her?* He opened his mouth to speak, and Chief held out his hand to quiet him for the second time.

"I have spoken. Come first light, you will both leave." With that, Gray Owl stood and left the wigwam.

Shane sat for some time with his mouth ajar. *What the hell did I just get myself into? I can't marry Tia.* A million reasons ran through his mind why he shouldn't do this. He could just hop on his bike and get the hell away from the camp, but how would he live with himself if he did that? Shane stretched out on his makeshift bed and closed his eyes. The vision of Kelly rose in his mind, the same vision he'd experienced the night by the fire. She smiled her unforgettable smile and repeated her wish for him to keep his heart open and that she was okay. *I'll do it and I will win. After that, I will set Tia free to do as she wishes.* Maybe he'd take her back home so both of them could be free to love whomever they chose, whether it was someone new or their deceased spouses.

Shane sat up. His plan just might work. He'd better find Tia and explain to her exactly what his intentions were. He didn't want her to think he had an ulterior motive. Raven wasn't going to be pleased with this turn of events. Shane got to his feet and headed out of the wigwam. He saw no sign of the Chief or Raven. He did see Tia still helping her mother clean the fish.

Half way to them, Raven stepped out of nowhere and blocked his path. His nostrils flared and he breathed heavily.

"Tia will be my wife," he growled. "I will win tomorrow, and you will leave here and not come back."

Shane planted his feet firmly on the ground and straightened. He stared right into Raven's black eyes. "We shall see who wins. In fact, when *I win*, you will let Tia decide for herself. Agreed?" Shane held out his hand.

Raven's upper lip curled back in a sneer. He moved a mere inch from Shane's face. As he spoke, spit landed on Shane's face. "You are not welcome here. Why do you come and think you know more than we do? I will show you I am the better man. Tia will be my wife and give me a child."

Shane had never backed down before and was not about to start doing so now. "If I were you I wouldn't be too quick to start planning a wedding. You have no idea who I am or what I am capable of. Trust me, the best man *will* win."

His whole body trembled with rage. He turned, leaving the big angry native to stand alone, but changed his direction, thinking it best to calm down before talking to Tia. He saw her watching them. She looked scared and confused.

Raven thinks he has this whole race in the bag. This isn't a game of cowboys and Indians. Shane smirked. *We're playing bikers and natives now, big guy, and everyone knows that bikers always play to win.*

Chapter Twelve

Tia watched Shane stomp off after his confrontation with Raven. Obviously they were both pretty angry about something, and if her instincts were correct, that something had to do with her. Why did this white man care so much about her having to marry someone she didn't love? Did he simply feel sorry for her and understand her pain?

Danti had been the most beautiful spirit she'd ever known. She remembered when he announced they should marry. Her heart sang like the birds welcoming the first wakening of spring. Most of her friends in the camp had their husbands chosen by their fathers. Some of them were happy and had learned to love the men their fathers had chosen for them. Others turned cold and bitter, going about their wifely duties, rarely smiling.

First, she and Danti had to convince her father they should marry. It hadn't been too difficult because Chief liked Danti. Everybody liked Danti, yet he chose her to be his wife. Once again, her love's death brought tears to her eyes. She pursed her lips and breathed deeply. *Now is not the time.* Releasing her pent up breath, she shuddered. Once she finished hanging the fish to dry, she'd try to find out exactly what happened—even if it meant talking to Raven.

"You look troubled, child." Elder Kaya took Tia's hand in her own and squeezed. "Come sit with me. It has been some time since we have talked."

Tia gazed into the wise old eyes of Danti's mother. The two had been quite close when Danti was alive. It was difficult for Tia to look at this woman who had been nothing but kind to her, for she shared the same eyes as her son.

"Too long," replied Tia. She smiled and joined Kaya next to the fire. "How have you been?"

"These old bones give me nothing but trouble." She shrugged, rubbing her knees. "No sense in complaining. It won't make them ache any less."

"I'm sorry, Kaya. Is there something I can do to help?"

"It is not me who needs help. I see something is troubling you, am I right?"

Kaya's deep brown eyes seemed to be looking past her gaze and into her innermost thoughts. Uncomfortable discussing her confusion with the mother of her dead husband, Tia took a deep breath and replied, "It is nothing for you to worry about, Kaya."

"You let me be the judge of what I worry about and what I don't," said the elder sternly. The twinkle in her eyes betrayed the tone of her voice.

Tia sighed. Tears threatened to escape and she diverted her gaze. "It has been some time since Danti passed. You have heard I am told I must marry again?"

"Yes. Raven is a very different man from our Danti."

Tia nodded, keeping her gaze trained on the ground.

"You do not wish to marry him. I can see there might be someone else that has taken a place in your heart." The corners of her mouth lifted in a knowing smile.

"How do you know this?" Tia should have known better than to try to keep anything from an elder. "I don't know how I feel right now, Kaya."

"I think you do." Kaya gathered Tia in her arms and smoothed her hair. "Do not think you are disrespecting Danti by loving another. He would want you to be happy."

The warmth of Kaya's embrace coaxed her tears to fall. How did she always know exactly what she needed to hear? Elder Kaya rocked her in her arms for some time without speaking. All around them, the camp carried on with their daily routines. The sounds of spring seemed to keep the rhythm of the tune she hummed softly into her hair. It was as if this woman who had loved her like her own child had somehow transmitted a gentle calmness to her spirit and made all of her confusion and unease take flight with the ocean breeze.

* * *

Shane walked at a brisk pace, trying to defuse his anger. There had to be some way to ensure that he won the race. Nothing would please him more than taking Raven's arrogant ego down a notch or two. Shane was more determined than ever to make sure Tia didn't marry that goon.

How the hell did you get yourself in this mess? Shane replayed the events of the past few weeks in his mind. It all seemed surreal. *I'm the only one I know who can get myself smack dab in the middle of something so bizarre.* He shook his head in disbelief. Spotting a tree up ahead of him, he walked over and sat down in its shade.

Sarsaparilla. Noni had given him Sarsaparilla tea and dressed his knuckles with it too. Looking down at his hands, he had undisputed evidence of how well it worked. Except for the pink of new skin, no one would ever know how badly he'd damaged his hands. No wonder the chief wanted to keep a supply of it on hand. *To think something so powerful is also the base for root beer.* He grinned.

Tomorrow, he'd head off into the highlands. Raven probably already knew exactly how to get there. He'd ask around camp for directions. Surely someone would be willing to help him out. Given Raven's sunny disposition, it wouldn't surprise him if he had a few enemies in the group. Thinking about it, Shane couldn't remember ever seeing him amongst the groups of jovial men who worked together.

Shane heard footsteps. He looked up to see Tia coming his way. He wondered if she knew about the race. He waved, and she waved back.

Tia sat down next to him and fixed her skirt around her. "What were you and Raven talking about?"

"I guess I might as well be the one who tells you." He shifted so that he faced her. "Your father and I had a little talk. It seems Raven is none too happy about our friendship."

"It is none of his business who I am friends with. I am not his wife... yet." Color rose in her cheeks, and she sat up on her knees. "What did my father say?"

"Well, I told your father how I felt about you being forced to marry a man you don't love." He braced himself for her reaction. "Your father has come up with a race of sorts to settle things once and for all."

"I don't understand."

"Tomorrow morning, we'll leave at first light to find sarsaparilla. Whoever brings it home first wins."

"Wins?" Tia looked confused; her brow knitted. "Wins what?"

Shane looked her in the eye. "You."

Her jaw dropped. She frantically searched Shane's eyes. "You win me? You can't be serious."

"It is the only way for you to get out of having to marry Raven."

"You don't love me. You are still in love with your wife!"

"And you are still in love with Danti." Shane heaved a sigh. "If I win, I don't expect you to marry me, Tia. I'm hoping your father will let you make your own choice. If it's the only way, then I'll be willing to marry you. At least you will be able to grieve your husband in peace."

Tia's eyes filled with tears and spilled down her honeyed cheeks. Her lips quivered. "Why would you do this for me?"

"For a number of reasons. Mainly because I think it's wrong that you're forced to marry—especially a man like Raven." Shane took her hand in his. "I'll never make you do anything you don't want to do. I can't offer you much except friendship. Maybe one day we'll be in a place where we see things differently. You're a beautiful woman, Tia, and if things were different, I'd be crazy not to want to marry you. My heart belongs to Kelly, and yours to Danti. Maybe we can help each other get through the pain."

"You are an amazing man, Shane." Tears ran freely now, and her voice grew thick with emotion. "Raven has lived in these mountains all his life. How can you expect to win this race?"

"Don't underestimate me." Shane winked. "All I need to know is the best way to get to your uncle's village. Do you know where I need to go?"

Tia smiled broadly, a small glimmer of hope in her deep brown eyes. "When Danti was here, my father sent him for it. My father always said he didn't understand how he brought it so quickly. Most men took a full day and night to go and come back. Danti would leave at first light and be home before the sun set."

"Please tell me you know the path he took."

"I do." She beamed at him.

Shane sat for some time with Tia under the tree. She told him of the path Danti used to take. She also told him the path in which Raven would probably go. Raven would be on horseback, so he'd be able to travel through parts Shane couldn't. For the first time all day, Tia offered him a genuine smile. "Raven would never suspect you would know a faster way. In fact, he is probably thinking he's already won the race."

"We can't raise his suspicions. Tonight, you will not talk to me at all. I want you to act like you are angry about the race. Not only angry at your father and Raven, but at me too."

Tia giggled. "This will be fun. How can I thank you?"

"There's no need for thanks, Tia. I'm just doing what I feel is right." He patted her hand before standing. "I think you should go back now. I'll wait a while before I make an appearance. Do you think you can handle our ruse?"

"I will play the part so well that even you will think I am angry at you." Tia laughed devilishly.

Her laughter sounded like music to Shane's ears. He found himself chuckling too. "Go on, then!" Shane shooed her away.

Later, on his way back to camp, Shane strolled along in the shadow of a massive row of evergreens that lined the precipice above the ocean. He needed to make sure enough time passed before making an appearance. To pull off their ruse, they'd have to be very careful. If Raven even remotely suspected they were up to something, he'd be tripping all over himself to tell the chief.

His stomach growled in anticipation of the wonderful smells wafting on the breeze. Since coming to the camp, he'd eaten some of the best food he'd ever tasted. The women busied themselves around the fires as he made his way to his wigwam. He smiled gratefully, noticing a pan over a fire and filled with simmering meat and vegetables.

Balancing a plate on his knees, he pierced a chunk of meat from it. The succulent morsel fell apart in his mouth. Without looking too obvious, he scanned the various clusters of natives eating their meals. The Chief, Noni, and Tia sat together by one of the many fires. Shane stifled a laugh upon seeing the pout on Tia's face. She sat with her back to her parents. Gray Owl looked up from his plate and glanced in her direction.

Quickly, Shane polished off the entire plate of food. He noticed Noni and Chief sat smoking pipes, but Tia had left her seat. In front of Raven's wigwam, the big native sat alone, sopping up his plate with a crust of bread. Shane wondered why he always seemed to be alone. Was he that terrible that the other men refused to spend any time with him?

Shane stood up and stretched his arms above his head. With his belly full, he suddenly felt very lethargic. If he didn't find something to do soon, he'd be sleeping before the sun set. He walked over to Noni and the Chief. Without being obvious, maybe he could discover where Tia had gone.

"Hello," said Shane, taking a seat next to Noni. "Thank you for supper. It was delicious."

"You are welcome." Noni said, rising from her seat. She gathered the supper dishes and disappeared around the side of the wigwam.

"Would you like to smoke?" asked Gray Owl, an ornery smirk on his face.

Shane laughed. "I think I'll pass. Thanks just the same."

"My daughter is very angry with me at the moment."

"I'm sorry to hear that. Is she angry with me too?" Shane hoped his voice didn't convey his nervousness.

"Tia is angry at the world right now. She would not even talk to me." Chief shrugged his shoulders. "Women. Sometimes I do not understand them."

"You and every other red-blooded male, Chief."

Chief nodded in agreement.

An amiable silence fell between them. Chief puffed on his pipe, and Shane feigned interest in a group of children kicking a ball back and forth. His mind went over the route Tia had explained to him earlier. It would be about a three-hour ride to reach the highlands. The route Raven would take led him through the trees. From what he understood, Raven would be on horseback. How ironic that Shane would be on his *ironhorse*.

Shane watched Raven exit the outhouse. *Good, he's not with Tia, but, where could she be?* On cue, she rounded the wigwam. She stopped dead in her tracks, her angry gaze piercing Shane. Pursing her lips, she stomped her foot and spun on her heel, heading back the direction she'd just come.

Chief chuckled. "I guess that answers your question."

Shane arched an eyebrow and rolled his eyes. "Can't win for losing some days."

* * *

Tia clamped a hand over her mouth to stifle a giggle. She hadn't expected to find Shane sitting with her father. Luckily, she thought quickly, knowing how important it was to have them all think her angry. She still couldn't believe Shane would do this for her. Relief filled her entire being that she would not have to marry Raven. Shane just *had* to win the race.

Grabbing the empty water buckets from behind the wigwam, Tia strolled down the path towards the water. Her heart sang with elation, inspiring her to sing vocally, but she dare not. One could never know who would be on this path or down by the water. She imagined a few of the women doing exactly what she intended to do. Fill buckets, one for dishes and the other to heat so they could wash up before bed.

A tall shadow loomed over her. A sense of loathing washed over her, telling her who it was before she looked. Quickly remembering her ploy, she glared at him and turned her head away. Her heart pounded so loudly that he must surely hear it.

"It is not me you should be angry with," he snarled. "The white man is the one causing all the trouble. Everything was fine before he got here."

"Fine for you maybe," she hissed. She kept her expression stony.

Raven wrapped his hand around her arm and pulled her to a stop. She defiantly turned her face away, but felt his hot breath against her cheek. His body emanated anger as he whispered in her ear. "You *will* be my wife, Tia, and we *will* have a child. This I promise." He brushed his lips against her cheek before stepping back and giving her a slight push, almost causing her to lose her balance.

At that moment, Tia had never hated anyone as much as she hated Raven. She looked up at the man who her father had chosen for her. A slow smile spread across her face, and turning, she continued down the path. He growled in their native tongue, barely loud enough for her to hear. It didn't take a genius to translate the tone of his voice. If, by chance, Shane didn't win the race, she knew Raven would take great pleasure in asserting his husbandly rights. Bile rose in her throat. The thought of him on top of her made her gag.

Tonight, she would burn sage to drive out all the anger Raven brought to her and the rest of her people, including Shane. Afterwards, she would burn sweetgrass to welcome good in its place. Also, while everyone slept, she would sneak into Shane's tent to sprinkle cedar chips in his fire and ask Glooscap to watch over him on his journey.

Since she was a little girl, Tia had been taught that Glooscap stood for all that is good and right. Surely he wouldn't want her to marry Raven, who stood for evil. Perhaps this was a test to see how much faith she had. She reached the water's edge. Setting down her buckets, she knelt, cupped the clear, cool water in her hands, and raised them toward the sky. The liquid trailed down her arms.

Good and mighty Glooscap. Hear my plea. Keep the white man, Shane, safe and out of harm's way. May all that is good prevail in the coming days—hear my plea.

Tia filled her buckets and carried them back to camp, readying herself for a fight. Each time she heard a noise, she'd stoop suddenly and look around, causing water to slosh over the sides of the buckets. She'd always been told she had a feisty spirit. Danti used to joke about her fearlessness. He often told her that if she ever ran into a grizzly, it would know to run the other way. Raven, however, wasn't a grizzly. He was a... Tia didn't know what to compare him to except an unclean spirit. Something in Raven's eyes left a rather unsettling feeling in the pit of her stomach.

One of the women from camp headed towards her with a pail of soiled diapers. She'd just given birth to a baby girl a few months ago. Dark circles stained the skin under her eyes. The baby's cries filled the camp each night. Tia felt sorry for the new mother, her obvious lack of sleep wearing her down more. Her husband, a hard and angry man, never helped her with anything. Amongst her people, the women had the sole responsibility of caring for the children. The men were responsible for protecting the family and providing meat and fish to eat.

"Hi Onawa." Tia smiled at her tired friend.

She looked up from the path, returning the smile.

"How is Mika doing? Is she finally able to sleep through the night?"

Onawa shook her head and frowned. "I wish," she sighed. "I think she has her days and nights mixed up."

Only a year younger than her friend, Tia noticed a bit of gray had begun to streak Onawa's hair. The poor girl had been chosen to marry a man much like Raven. At one time, Onawa and Tia had been the best of friends. That is, until she married. The woman who stood before her, a mere skeleton of the person she'd been, made Tia's heart ache. She mirrored her own future as Raven's wife.

"Can I help?" Tia asked.

"Thank you, but this is my only time where Mika's grandma watches her so I can do her wash. I like to make it last a long time." She chuckled tiredly.

Tia smiled. "Well, enjoy your time away, then."

The two women parted ways with a nod of their heads. Seeing Onawa reaffirmed her decision that no matter how the race ended, she would not marry Raven. Even if it meant running away from her people, she'd do it. What kind of life would she have if she submitted and married him? She'd rather live alone than sentence her future with the likes of him.

At the top of the path, Noni waited for her. By the way she stood with her hands on her hips, Tia saw she wasn't very happy. She hurried towards her and took one of the pails.

"Do you think I have nothing better to do than wait for you? Soon it will be too dark to do our chores," Noni snapped, hurrying up the path ahead of her daughter. "Honestly, Tia, I don't know what's gotten into you lately."

Being forced to marry an animal like Raven is what's getting to me, Tia wanted to scream. *You're my mother. Why don't you take a stand for me? Can you not see what is going on?* She knew her mother couldn't do anything about the situation even if she wanted to. She knew her mother well enough that she must have thoughts about it all. Why had she not spoken to her about such things? Tia bit her lower lip. *Father, of course. He has forbidden her to discuss it with me.*

Chapter Thirteen

Shane had grown accustomed to the sun waking him up. Instead, he looked up at a dark and dreary sky. An occasional raindrop landed on the fire with a hiss. Seconds after Shane opened his eyes he got up and dressed. Today he'd been given the opportunity to put that asshole Raven in his place. He grinned, very much looking forward to the day.

He opened the flap and looked up at the sky. Dark, brooding clouds loomed overhead and threatened to burst open in a torrent of rain. Riding in a downpour wasn't only dangerous, it also hurt, but Shane enjoyed riding in a light rain. Imagine tiny pellets hitting your skin at sixty miles an hour.

A small group of people stood under a canopy suspended by the chief's wigwam. As soon as they saw that Shane had awakened, everyone ran towards his wigwam. Luckily, he managed to duck back inside before they plowed him over. Seconds before the first person entered, he pulled his bed and clothing over against the wall and straightened.

Shane stood back and watched each one take a place around the fire. One of the women added wood to the low embers. Taking her shawl off her head, she fanned the red coals into a crackling blaze. Some smiled his way upon entering; others talked amongst themselves as if he didn't exist.

A woman carried a pot of coffee over. Smiling shyly, she poured a cup and handed it to Shane. He gratefully accepted it and walked over to sit on his bed.

Finally the flap opened to show Chief Gray Owl and Noni. Seconds later, Tia followed. The Chief and Noni's expressions were serious. Tia frowned, her dark eyes a raging storm. *She's either been arguing with her parents or is an excellent actor. By the looks of Chief and Noni, I'd wager they've had one doozy of a fight.*

Chief Gray Owl sat in his usual place, his eyes scanning those present until they came to rest on Shane. He motioned him over. Shane held out his cup to the friendly woman, who made her rounds with the pot.

"Thank you." Shane said, amused at the color that tinged her cheeks. He got up carefully, so as not to upset his coffee and sat next to the Chief. "Good Morning."

Raven entered the wigwam. His brooding presence inspired an uncomfortable hush over the people. Upon noticing Shane sitting next to the chief, his eyes flashed with anger. He turned on his heel and left.

"I don't think he likes me." Shane grinned.

"This is not a joke. His reputation amongst friends and family is on the line," Chief spoke sternly. "You forget, you can leave any time you choose.

This is Raven's home no matter the outcome of this race."

"I know that, Chief. Don't forget we're talking about your daughter's happiness as well," snapped Shane. He didn't want the chief to be on the receiving end of all his pent up frustration. Suddenly the wigwam seemed very small. "I need some air." Without waiting for a response, he stood and left, feeling all eyes follow him across the room. At this particular point in time, he couldn't have cared less. He just needed to get out—now.

Shane bounded through the opening. His foot caught the bottom edge of the flap. He fell, landing in a huge puddle. He looked down at his mud covered hands and knees.

Perfect...just fucking perfect!

He grumbled all the way to his bike. It rained just enough to keep the ground slick. A couple times, he almost kissed the ground again. Opening his saddlebag, he took out a change of clothes. From the other saddlebag, he removed his rain suit. Shane stood holding the clothing in his arms, wondering where he could go to change.

Like I have any other options. Shrugging, he trudged through mud towards the small outhouse. It would take some fancy maneuvering for him to get changed in there. Like Clark Kent entering a phone booth, Shane stepped into the outhouse. Although not Superman, Shane stepped out minutes later dressed in all his riding gear.

In the short amount of time it took to get dressed, it had stopped raining. Behind the ominous clouds, the sky shone bright with the promise of a better day. Shane couldn't wait to go for a ride. People started leaving the wigwam, including Tia. Briefly, she looked his way and shot him a knowing smile. Finally, the chief emerged with Noni in tow.

Sitting tall and proud, Raven rode a black stallion past a gathering of majestic evergreens to the Chief, who now sat outside smoking his pipe. In one fluid movement, he dismounted and loosely tied his mount to a tree.

Raven stood before the chief, his muscle-bound arms crossed over his thick chest. The feathers in his hair and a matching deerskin shirt and fringed pants made him a formidable presence. In contrast, Shane stood next to him, wearing jeans, black leather boots, and a jacket. He kept his focus on the Chief.

"You know what has been asked of you? Raven, you know of the sarsaparilla?" Chief waited until he nodded. He reached in the large over-sized pocket of his poncho-style coat and pulled out a plant—roots and all. About two feet long, it boasted long-stalked leaves, with pointed sections. White flowers clustered on rounded umbels bloomed on each separate stalk. Where the two stalks joined, six small, blue-black berries hung. "This is sarsaparilla. As you both know, it is very powerful medicine. Not only does it heal cuts and burns, it is used to calm and to help one sleep; it also aids our elders when the harsh winter gives them chest colds." Chief paused, inhaling the smoke from his pipe. "What you might not know, Shane, is that the white man once used the berries to make *root beer*. This is why sarsaparilla only grows in certain places that are now protected from harvesting.

"I have sent word to my good friend and brother, Chief White Wolf. He is expecting you. He will only give the supply of sarsaparilla to the one who reaches him first. Do you have any questions?" Chief finished, looking from Raven to Shane.

"No," said Raven.

Shane shook his head and inhaled the now familiar aroma of sage. He watched Noni set fire to it in a shallow stone bowl. In her other hand, she held a long feather similar to the ones in Raven's hair. Chanting in her native tongue, she closed the distance between her and Raven. She fanned the feather over the bowl and pushed the pungent smoke towards him. He cupped his hands, scooping the smoke and spreading it from the top of his head down to his toes. He bowed his head reverently, and Noni spoke a few final words before moving to Shane.

"Allow this burning cedar to fill your senses," chanted Noni. "It will fill you with the promise of a safe journey."

Shane wasn't sure if he believed any of it. He did, however, respect Noni and rather than possibly offending her, he followed her instructions. Shane bowed his head, and Noni repeated the same words spoken over Raven. Finished, she returned to her place beside the chief.

"You leave now. Remember, the first man back will decide Tia's future." Chief Gray Owl stood and shook first Raven's hand and then Shane's. "May Glooscap watch over you both."

Raven and Shane separated. *Where is Tia?* Surely she watched from a hidden place. He looked up at the sky, happy to see the gray clouds moving away. Sunlight filtered down through patches of blue. At this rate, he'd be riding on dry roads in no time. The paths through the trees would dry slowly, giving him a bit of an advantage over Raven who would ride through wet foliage and over slippery ground.

He rolled up his rain suit and tucked it back into his saddlebag. Standing over Belle, he came down with all his weight and was rewarded by a loud rumble. He settled on his seat and slipped on his half gloves. Shane raised the kickstand with his foot and popped the bike into gear.

On his way down the lane, he saw Tia behind the trunk of a tall cedar.

She raised her hand in farewell before turning and disappearing amongst the trees.

Shane smiled, happy to have seen her before leaving. It reaffirmed the reasons for his quest. With renewed fervor, he twisted the throttle and headed for the highlands.

* * *

Shane couldn't have asked for a nicer day to ride in the wind. The clouds had parted to reveal a most stupendous blue sky. All around him, nature celebrated life. Birds soared above him, and in the ocean to his left, dolphins played a game of tag. After losing Kelly, days like this kept him going.

The mid morning sun kissed his face, but the heat penetrating his black leather jacket made him hot and uncomfortable. Looking for a place to pull over, he saw the familiar black stallion standing on the side of the road. Shane slowed down and scanned the bush for Raven. He frowned and sighed, pulling over a few yards away from the horse that stood munching on some tall grass. Taking off his jacket, Shane tucked it in his saddlebag and started walking up the road.

Shane kept his guard up. He wouldn't put it past Raven to try and lure him into a trap that would keep him from winning the race. Easing up to the horse, Shane spoke gently and reached out. The horse sniffed at him, snorted softly, and resumed eating.

"Good boy," said Shane. He rubbed the horse between its ears. "Now where is Raven?" He walked into the brush a little ways. *Strange. The horse isn't even tied up. This doesn't look good.* Before going any further, he hiked back to the horse and tied him off to a tree. "Be good." Shane patted his neck and walked in the woods in search of his rival.

I should just get on my bike and leave. No matter how tempting it might be, he just couldn't do such a thing. With his luck, he'd probably find the gorilla hunkered down behind a tree taking a dump. Shane snapped off a long, thin branch and started hitting the ground in front of him. If there was one thing he hated, it was a snake. One hiss, or a wiggle under his foot, and he'd be screaming like a girl back to his bike.

"Raven? Are you out here?" He paused to listen. Silence greeted him. He doubted Raven had come through the thick brush with the horse, so he stuck to the path and walked on a little further before stopping again. "Raven? If you can hear me, then holler!" Something was seriously wrong. Either that, or Raven was on his horse, listening and laughing as he rode away.

Fuck this! He isn't going to pull one over on me.

A faint noise reached him. Standing perfectly still, he strained to listen. He couldn't make out what or where the sound came from. Just up ahead, the path veered off to the right. The sound, however, seemed to come from the bushes on the other side.

"Raven? Are you out there?" Shane shouted again.

"I'm over here! Help me!"

Shane hurried over in the direction of the cry. The swampy ground made it difficult to walk. It was like walking with suction cups strapped to his boots.

He untangled a jumble of vines and branches to get closer to the voice. *How the hell did he get back here?* A branch whipped back and sliced his cheek.

"Holy shit!" His gloved hand flew to his cheek and came away wet.

"Hey!" Raven's voice reached him. "Are you still out there?"

Shane swiped the remaining foliage out of his way and stopped short, narrowly escaping the same demise as Raven. Laughter burst from Shane.

In the center of a massive mud pool, buried to his waist, stood Raven.

Shane steadied himself, took a couple steps back, and lost the last of his restraint. Doubled over, gasping for breath, he laughed like he'd never laughed before. Tears rolled down his face as he watched Raven grow madder and madder.

"Are you going to just stand there all day laughing at me, or are you going to help me out of this mess?"

The mud splattered on his face looked like a tomato gone bad. He noted branches and rocks lying scattered by his feet, but nothing that would handle Raven's weight. After a final assessment of the situation, he turned to leave.

"Where do you think you are going? You can't leave me here like this," yelled Raven.

Shane chuckled to himself and kept moving without saying a word. *It won't hurt the asshole to think I'm leaving him here.* He'd have to bring back the horse and find something to tie to Raven to drag him out of the mud pit.

Luckily for Raven, Shane discovered a rope hanging from the side of the saddle. He decided to play it safe and walk the steed to the pit. The only horse he'd ever ridden had been an ironhorse. Maybe today wasn't the best of days to learn how to ride a living, breathing one.

By the time he made it back to Raven, he'd sunk even deeper into the pit. He held his hands out to his sides, the mud up to his armpits. He no longer looked ready to kill; he now appeared downright scared. The slightest movement sucked him down further. Shane coiled the rope around his forearm and tied one end around the stallion's neck.

"I'm going to lasso you, so don't try to catch the rope. You'll just end up sinking more. Wait until the rope is around you, then grab hold, and your horse will pull you out."

Raven took a slow, deep breath and nodded. Shane's first lasso attempt landed a couple feet behind the man. He imagined Raven biting his tongue. The second attempt hit him but didn't go around him. Finally, on the third try, the rope landed around his head.

The big man latched onto the rope with both hands. Shane stepped back beside the horse and slowly led him up the path. The stallion's neck muscles strained against the weight, but he steadily moved forward. Shane followed the length of the rope back to the edge of the pit. With feet firmly planted on the ground, he pulled.

He felt the weight lessen as Raven made his way over the edge. The big Indian clawed at the ground, pulling himself the rest of the way out. He lay on his back at Shane's feet and gasped for air, his entire body slathered in mud. The rope tightened, his horse snorting from the path. It would take him a while to recover and clean the mud from his clothes. Other than that, he'd be fine.

"So, tell me, how the hell did you end up in the pit?"

Raven opened his eyes and looked up at Shane. "My horse spooked and he threw me. That's where I landed."

Shane refrained from laughing. "Talk about bad luck." He shook his head. "Well, I'm glad you're okay, but I must be going. I have some plants to pick up for the chief."

Raven's eyes blazed. "You can't leave me like this!"

"I can and I will. I may have just saved your life, but that doesn't mean you're not still an asshole. See you at the finish line."

Feeling very pleased with himself, he made his way back to his bike. Just to be sure he heard him leaving, he sat on Belle and gave her plenty of gas. It would be a good hour before Raven was in any shape to continue on the journey. By then, Shane would be at their destination and hopefully on his way back home.

Chapter Fourteen

After Shane rode out of her line of vision and she could no longer hear the sound of the ironhorse's powerful engine, Tia wandered back to camp. The men prepared to go fishing, and most of the women sat making birch bark wall hangings to sell at the market.

Once a month, during the busiest time of island tourism, her camp filled their pickup trucks and headed to Langley, where vendors from all over gathered to sell their wares. In just one day, they would make enough money to buy the supplies needed to wait out the long winter months in their winter homes.

With her mind still on the two men who'd just left camp, Tia didn't feel like she would be able to concentrate on her tasks. At least she didn't have to worry about Raven pulling any dirty tricks since he took a different route.

Tia decided to go for a swim to burn off some of the nervousness. She'd do her chores later. Once she'd gathered a change of clothes, she walked toward the path to the water. She passed Onawa sitting by the fire out front of her wigwam.

"Is Mika sleeping?" asked Tia.

Onawa looked up from the small pair of pants she mended and smiled. "Yes, she'll be good for at least an hour."

"How about going for a swim with me?"

Onawa looked surprised at the invitation. She glanced toward her wigwam and around the camp. "I can't tell you how good that sounds, but what if Mika wakes up?"

"I'll ask my mother to listen for her. She can call you if she does."

Onawa stood and put the pants down. Her smiled told how happy she was to be doing something just for her and not someone else. "Let me get my things."

"I'll be right back, then. I'll just go tell my mother to keep a look out for you."

"Thank you, Tia." Excitement danced in her eyes, and she ducked inside the wigwam.

Tia's mother thought it was a terrific idea for Onawa to have a break and gladly agreed to keep watch. In a matter of minutes, they began their walk down the path together.

"I can't remember the last time we did anything like this together." Tia smiled warmly.

Although obviously tired, Onawa smiled back and sighed. "You must be worried about the race today?"

"I think I'll go crazy waiting to see the outcome."

"I hope Raven loses the race," whispered Onawa, her gaze darting in all directions, as if she feared her words would be overheard.

"No matter who wins or loses, I will not marry him," Tia said. Saying the words out loud was empowering.

"How can you say that? If he wins, you can't go against your father's wishes." Concern etched her brow.

As they neared the sandy beach, blue water lapped at the shore. The sun's reflection sparkled on the rippling waves. Tia and Onawa set down their packs and began to undress.

"I am not going to marry Raven, Onawa. Even if it means leaving for good."

Onawa paused, her shirt half off, her mouth ajar. "Surely you wouldn't!"

"I don't want to, but if I have to...I will."

Tia stood naked beside her friend. They were very different in stature. Onawa had the womanly curves from having a child and Tia's stomach lay flat and hard. Where Tia's hair was dark and shiny, Onawa's lay limp, prematurely graying.

"I'll race you!" Tia laughed and started running toward the ocean.

Onawa stumbled out of the pants pooled around her ankles. "No fair, I wasn't ready."

They swam around for a while, splashing and laughing like they did while growing up together. Onawa made her way to the flat boulder first. She climbed on top and stretched out, smiling broadly.

"I am so out of shape," she said breathlessly.

Tia laughed and joined her friend. "This is heavenly."

"Mmm hmm."

"Tell me something, Tia." Onawa leaned on her elbow and rested her head on her hand.

"Sure."

"Does the white man have anything to do with your decision not to marry Raven?"

Tia opened her eyes and squinted against the sun. *Am I really so transparent? First Kaya, and now Onawa.* She sighed. "You know how much I loved Danti?"

Onawa nodded.

"It is so hard to sort out how I feel about Shane. It is different from how I felt about my husband." She groaned. "I'm not making any sense, am I?"

Onawa chuckled. "You are confused. Do you want to know what I think?"

"I'm not sure." Tia laughed nervously.

"I think you are feeling guilty for the way you think about the white man."

Tears sprung to Tia's eyes and she blinked them away. She swallowed hard before attempting to speak. "Why is love so difficult?"

Onawa rolled over on her back and looked up at the sky. "Be happy you have loved at all, my friend. Some of us aren't so lucky."

* * *

Given the turn of events, Shane pretty much had the race in the bag. As long as he didn't get lost trying to find Chief White Wolf, he'd stay right on track.

You'd think the asshole, Raven, would have at least said thanks for saving his sorry ass. Once an asshole, always an asshole.

According to Tia's instructions, he only had a short distance to go. She'd told him the camp sat closer to the road than theirs did and he should be able to see the village from the road. He'd never been this far into the highlands before and wasn't surprised to see it held the same beauty as the rest of the country he'd traveled. The traffic was sparse, which suited him just fine. It gave him time to think about the situation he'd gotten himself into.

Winning this race would free Tia from her father's promise of marriage to Raven. Would the chief actually expect them to marry? Why did it feel like he was cheating on Kelly?

Up ahead, two native women sat behind a crude stand. They sold wall hangings similar to the ones the women back at camp made with porcupine quills and birch bark. He slowed down and waved. Neither woman waved back, but they giggled behind their hands and turned away shyly.

Just past where they were set up, he saw small cabin-like structures sitting a few feet back from the road. A gravel lane led into their camp. Shane turned off onto the gravel and carefully made his way up to a camp twice the size of Gray Owl's.

A group of natives gathered to watch the arrival of the white man on a motorcycle. Unlike the women back at camp, they wore more modern clothing. Some wore dresses with aprons and others wore jeans and oversized shirts. The men were dressed like any other fisherman on the island.

The crowd separated as Shane got off his bike, and a tiny, frail looking man stepped forward. He smiled broadly, showing off a silver-capped tooth he seemed quite proud of. Unlike Chief Gray Owl, he wore jeans and a button-down shirt.

"Greetings. You must be my brother's friend, Shane. I am Chief White Wolf." He held out his bony hand.

Shane took his hand. "Hello. Yes, I'm Shane. I'm told that you have some sarsaparilla for me to take back to the chief?"

Chief White Wolf didn't acknowledge his question. He turned his attention to Shane's motorcycle and walked past him for a closer look.

"Careful, the pipes are still hot," said Shane, feeling a bit mystified.

"So this is the machine my brother is learning to ride?" he asked and glanced at him over his shoulder.

"Yes. Your brother's a fast learner."

White Wolf walked around the bike studying every detail. He paused, reached out, and touched the bell. "Why is this bell here?"

Shane wasn't sure how to answer. "It was a...gift." He hoped his answer satisfied the man's curiosity enough that he'd drop the subject.

"I have heard about the evil road spirits. We will have tea and talk."

"I don't want to sound ungrateful, but I really must be going. I'm sure your brother told you of the race?" The last thing Shane wanted was to hear stories of evil spirits.

Chief White Wolf nodded. "Yes, he told me. Now, come and have a quick cup of tea with me."

Shane didn't want to make the old man angry for fear he wouldn't get the plants he'd come for. "All right...a quick one. I'm sure Raven isn't far behind me."

The chief clapped happily and waved for Shane to follow him. "Come with me. My Ada will pour us some tea."

Reluctantly, he followed the chief to one of the many fires that littered the village. Gesturing towards the fire, White Wolf offered Shane a seat on a plastic lawn chair. Shane sat down next to the chief, and a short, stout woman poured them each a cup of tea. A familiar smell wafted up and he took a sip to confirm it was indeed mint.

"So how did you come across this bell?" asked the chief.

"I really don't remember. It was so long ago," he lied, not wanting to discuss the bell with this strange little man.

The Chief looked at him through dark, penetrating eyes that made Shane squirm in his seat. Nervously, he drank the hot tea down in one gulp, which scolded his tongue and throat. Standing up, he set the cup on the ground next to the chair.

"Thank you for the tea. I really must be leaving."

"Whoever gave you this bell must have thought you'd come in contact with evil road spirits." The chief's gaze bored into him.

His words stopped Shane in his tracks. His heart beat wildly as he waited for the man to continue.

"The belief is that the evil spirits will become trapped inside the bell. The constant ringing will drive them insane, making them lose their grip until they fall to the ground."

"Where did you learn about the legend?"

"Riders of the ironhorse are not the first to use the bell. My ancestors used silver beads, not unlike the bell of today. They put them around the necks of the steeds believed to be possessed by demons. Once the spooked horse heard the rhythm of the beads, the animal became a pleasure to ride."

Shane's skin prickled with unease. All he wanted to do was get as far away from this man as soon as possible.

"You must go now. I will have Ada bring the plants to your motorcycle." White Wolf smiled and nodded. "Safe journey, and remember, if you ever find yourself in trouble, all you need to do is ring the bell and he will come."

Shane didn't need to be told twice. Without looking back, he hurried towards his bike. There was something eerie and unsettling about this camp. Right now, his focus needed to be on Tia and getting back to camp before Raven.

With helmet and gloves on, he sat on his bike ready to make a quick get away. Finally, Ada hurried to him carrying a large wicker box.

Terrific! How the hell am I going to take that on my bike?

He got off of Belle and took the box from Ada. She smiled and left him alone. Luckily, he always carried a couple of Bungee cords in his saddlebags. He strapped the box down on his passenger seat. Within minutes, he kicked the Shovelhead to life. Twisting the throttle, he tore down the short lane and out onto the main road. He never looked back.

What is it with the Micmac's chiefs?

The last thing he expected today was a discussion about the friggin' bell hanging on his bike. He just wanted to return to camp with the sarsaparilla and be done with the whole marriage deal.

Shane purposely passed the place where he'd spotted Raven's horse. He slowed down and looked in every direction. On the ground lay piles of drying horseshit, and by the looks of the large amount of mud caked on the road, Raven had one hell of time cleaning off before he'd left. Smiling broadly, Shane sped on down the road.

It had been awhile since he rode the Shovelhead wide open. A surge of adrenaline shot through his veins. Up ahead, he saw a wide bend in the road. Maintaining his speed, he leaned into the curve. A trail of sparks ignited as his floorboards hit the asphalt, jarring Shane from enjoying the ride. He'd flipped off kids for riding their crotch rockets the way he just did.

Slowing down to a more respectable speed, he scolded himself. *You're going to get yourself killed, you old fool!*

Why should he be in such a hurry? He had the plants and only a few miles to go. What good would it do Tia if he ended up in pieces all over the road?

The sun set over the mountains, and memories began to stir in his mind. He remembered how excited Kelly had been the day she brought home the two humungous flower planters. She wouldn't let him have a moment's peace until he finally went outside and hauled the monstrosities off the back of the truck and put one on either side of the front door.

All night long she'd go to the window and stare with excitement in her eyes. God, he missed her zest for life, as it was quite infectious.

Would she be happy about what I'm doing for Tia?

He couldn't shake the nagging sense that in some way he was cheating on her. Kelly always told him to listen to his heart. She felt by doing so, one could never go wrong. He sighed. If only life were that simple.

The temperature dropped with the setting sun. He knew he should pull over and put on a jacket but he didn't. In less than an hour, he'd be back at camp. A roaring fire and a pot of stew simmering over it sounded like Heaven. His stomach growled at the thought of food. With everything that had happened today, he'd forgotten to eat.

Shane turned on his headlight and twisted the wick, climbing just a little above the speed limit. He smelled wood smoke and looked to either side of the road for signs of a fire. It wasn't uncommon for fires to spark in the mountains, although unlikely given the rain from that morning. Just off to his right, he saw smoke curling up through a cluster of evergreens. Slowing to a crawl, he peered into the brush for the source of the smoke.

His curiosity got the best of him and he pulled over on the shoulder. A shiver rippled through him, and he got off the bike to rummage through the saddlebag for his jacket. He slid into the comfort of his well-worn leather before venturing off in search of the fire. Time was of the essence.

The smell of burning wood grew stronger as he pushed his way through the brush. He leaned against a tree trunk and pulled back a hanging branch.

By a roaring fire, and with his back to him, sat Sam.

For whatever reason, the hairs on the back of Shane's neck stood on end. Rather than make his presence known, he decided to leave unannounced. He didn't have time for a confrontation anyhow.

"Shane."

He turned, stopping dead in his tracks.

"Shane, please don't go. I mean you no harm."

"I have to go," Shane shouted over his shoulder and quickened his pace. There was something unsettling about Sam. If he did confront him, he'd rather it be by the light of day.

Shane emerged from the brush and jogged over to his bike. He checked his mirrors before pulling out onto the road. *Who the hell is that guy and why does he keep showing up every time I turn around?* He gave Belle a little gas and was happy when he started recognizing his surroundings. With a sigh of relief, he knew *home* was not too far now.

Now he needed to get through the next phase of the race and talk Chief into letting Tia make up her own mind—even if it meant she wanted to remain single and alone. He pulled his bike to a stop, and Tia ran across the grass towards him, grinning from ear to ear. His stop to help Raven, the strange little Chief, and his run in with the biker fell to the wayside. He barely made it off the bike before she launched herself into his arms, laughing and crying at the same time. He hugged her until her gasps subsided.

Tia stepped back, her cheeks stained pink. She looked down at the ground. "I...I'm sorry. It's been such a long day, and when I saw you riding up the road..."

"No need to explain, Tia. I'm ahead of Raven and that's all that matters now." Shane rested his hand on her shoulder. "Where's your father?"

"He went with the men to bring in their nets. You must be tired. Why don't I fix you a plate of supper and a hot cup of tea?"

"That's music to my ears darlin'." Shane's stomach growled in agreement. "What should I do with the sarsaparilla?"

"We will bring it to my mother and she will take care of it."

Shane untied the large wicker box and carried it on his hip, following Tia. She stopped in front of Shane's wigwam. "Why don't you wait in there while I get you some food? Nobody will bother you." She took the box from him and shifted the weight to her hip.

Shane smiled. "That's a great idea. Thanks, Tia."

"I should be the one thanking you for saving my life."

"Let's call it even." He smiled. "I'd really love a cup of tea."

"Of course! I'll be right back," she said, obviously flustered.

He watched her hurry away and laughed, but she heard him and turned. A small smile played at the corners of her mouth. She lowered her eyelashes and hurried away. Shane thought she looked like a little girl on Christmas morning full of excitement and not knowing which way to turn first. His body ached from riding all day. Opening the flap, he stepped inside. A crackling fire welcomed him.

His bed still lay where he'd left it pulled up against the wall, but now twice as many skins, plus his clothes, lay washed in a neat pile. It felt like coming home. He really enjoyed the Micmac's lifestyle. He wasn't too crazy about some of their beliefs, but he enjoyed their simple way of life.

Sitting down on the stump seat, he hiked up his foot and unlaced his mud-covered boots. He'd wash them off later; for now, he'd be happy just to take them off. He pulled and prodded, winced and cursed, and finally inched his boots off his swollen feet.

"Ahhhh," he moaned. Wiggling his toes, he grimaced. He exhaled heavily and switched legs to find the other foot just as difficult to set free. Finally, with both feet bare, he struggled to stand. He hobbled over to his bed and knelt, finding it easier to sit.

For a second, Shane lay back on his bed...just to catch his breath.

* * *

Tia hadn't been this happy in a very long time. Shane had won the race, and now she'd be set free. How would she ever be able to repay his kindness?

"Shane won the race, Mother."

Noni took the box from her, deep lines creasing her forehead.

"Aren't you happy?" asked Tia.

"I'm worried." She put down the box and took hold of Tia's hands. "I'm worried about what happens now."

Tia pulled her hands away and turned to leave. Humming a happy childhood tune, she filled a large bowl with the rabbit stew she'd cooked for the evening meal. With a chunk of cornbread and a mug of hot tea, she walked carefully over to his wigwam, dishes in hand.

"You will love the stew, Shane. I've been cooking it all day!" Tia looked over at him. He lay in an awkward position; she guessed he'd fallen asleep sitting up. Her heart pained for the man who had left in the wee hours of the morning on a mission to save her life.

Tia set down the tray and crept over to him. He lay snoring softly. She saw he'd managed to get his boots off, but his feet looked red and raw from wearing them all day. She rolled up one of the skins and set it at the bottom of his bed. Slowly and carefully, she picked up his feet and slid them on top of the bundle.

She scurried over to a covered pot on the other side of the wigwam and dipped her hand inside. With the same mixture her mother used to heal his hands, Tia carried some of the salve back to his sleeping form. She knelt by his feet and rubbed the salve over them. Tears sprung to her eyes; he had endured so much for her. Taking a larger skin, she covered his sleeping body and tucked it under his chin.

For a white man, he isn't too hard to look at. She brushed his hair back from his face.

"Thank you," she whispered, lightly brushing her lips on his forehead.

Tia left the tray on the stump and turned to leave. Pausing, she spotted his mud-covered boots by the fire. *What a mess. Surely they didn't get this way just from riding his ironhorse.* Taking the boots in one hand, she held them out in front of her and lifted the flap with the other. She stepped out just as Raven galloped into camp. Even in the darkness, she saw his eyes ablaze with anger and determination. Tia tried to duck back in the wigwam unnoticed, but he'd already spotted her.

"Now you are undressing the white man?" Raven bellowed from atop the filthy stallion. His horse breathed heavily, his flanks lathered.

"Of course not! He is sleeping now." Tia continued on her way.

Raven inched the stallion forward and blocked her path. "Do not think this is over, my sweet," he snarled. "You *will be* my wife. I don't care who made it back first."

"We'll see about that when my father returns." Tia slapped the horse's side hard enough that it whinnied and galloped off.

Raven cursed, "Bitch! You will see your father is not going to let you marry a white man. You know this is true!" His snide laughter taunted her.

Surely her father would not go back on his word? White man or not, her father had made a deal with Shane. Why would her father propose a race if nothing would change? In that moment, she hated Raven more than she'd ever hated another human being. She *would not* marry that evil man.

Chapter Fifteen

She woke alone in the wigwam that she shared with her parents. The morning sun's rays shone through the gap at the top. Wiping the sleep from her eyes, she jumped to her feet and hurriedly put on clean clothes. Tia left the wigwam, anxiously looking around camp for her father.

Her heart beat quickly as she ran to Shane's wigwam. She tore open the door to find an empty dwelling. Only the crackle of a dwindling fire greeted her. Her gaze rested on the empty dishes from the night before.

His boots!

Tia ran out to the spot where she'd cleaned his boots and found them still sitting there. Her eyes scanned the camp. Children sat in a circle with their teacher. Women made wall hangings or prepared fish for drying. She spotted her mother with a few women who cleaned fish and ran over and knelt beside her.

She tried to catch her breath. "Where is he?" she gasped.

Her mother looked at her and frowned. "What are you talking about?"

"Father...Shane... Where are they?" Tia fought tears.

"Calm down. Your father went fishing again this morning. As for Shane, I think he went for a swim. He asked for soap to wash his hair."

Tia breathed a sigh of relief.

"Raven is still sleeping. Now go make a pot of tea." She shooed her daughter away, shaking her head and griping to the other women about troublesome children.

Tia sauntered over to their cook fire and took the kettle off the grate. She filled a small bell-shaped vessel with holes full of their homemade tea mixture and set it in the bottom of the teapot. After pouring the hot water over the vessel, she set it back on the grate for steeping.

She decided to walk down to the water and perhaps have a chance to talk to Shane alone before her father returned, or Raven woke up. By the filthy shape in which Raven had arrived, and the mud-covered boots she'd cleaned for Shane, something had gone on during this race she hadn't been told about. She started down the steep incline to the water, paying close attention to the uneven path. By the time she thought of the possibility he might be bathing, it was too late.

Although he was unaware of her presence, Tia's jaw dropped at the sight of Shane floating spread-eagled in the water. The sun shone down on him and created a glistening effect on his naked form. Her hand flew to her mouth to stifle a gasp and she crouched down behind a cluster of bushes.

Her cheeks grew hot, and although thoroughly embarrassed, she couldn't tear her gaze away from him. She'd never seen a white man naked before. Brazenly, she studied the length of his long, lean frame. Except for the area his boxers or shorts covered when dressed, a dark tan covered Shane's skin. Native men hardly had any facial or body hair, unlike Shane who had a patch of curly dark hair covering his sleeping member. She eyed a sparse area of hair in the center of his chest and a trail leading down past his bellybutton, thickening as it progressed to his groin.

Since she'd met him, she'd never seen him with his hair loose. It now floated in the water around his head like a midnight halo. She noticed he'd shaved. In fact, she found her body growing warmer as she admired his nicely proportioned body. She'd only been with one man in her life and he looked nothing like Shane.

Guilt slipped over her at such carnal thoughts. She'd been a widow for almost a year. Not only did she miss Danti terribly, she also missed her wifely duties. Making love to her husband had not been the *duty* her mother and other elders spoke of. More often than not, she eagerly anticipated their time together alone.

Shane stood up in the water, startling Tia. Luckily, she caught herself before she yelped. If he caught her spying on him, how would she explain herself? Tia waited until Shane reached the shore, and the instant he turned to slip into his boxers, she made her move. Her foot caught a protruding root and she tumbled to the ground. She heard Shane's laughter. Mortified, heat flooded her cheeks.

Tia summoned up the courage to face him. After brushing the dirt from her knees, she turned to see him tucking his t-shirt in his jeans. She took a deep breath and made her way down the path.

"Fancy meeting you here," he chuckled. "If you had been a minute sooner, you might've caught me in an awkward position."

Words failed her. *So much for composure,* she thought as a fresh wave of heat assaulted her face. She watched him gather up his dirty clothes and shaving utensils.

"I take it your father isn't back from fishing?"

"No, not yet." She frowned. "I did see Raven when he rode in last night. He was covered from head to toe in mud. He says he will still marry me. Raven believes my father will never allow me to marry a white man."

Her bottom lip trembled and she fought the urge to cry.

"I think we should wait to talk to your father before jumping to conclusions. Maybe Raven is just a sore loser."

"Yes, of course, you are right. I put some tea on for you back at camp." Tia forced a smile and started on her way back to camp. "Are you hungry?"

"I'm always hungry." Shane followed her up the path. "Have you seen Raven yet this morning?"

Tia stopped and turned. "He's still sleeping and I'm in no hurry for him to wake up."

Shane took her hand and held it tightly. "You have nothing to fear. I promise that nothing will to happen to you as long as I'm around."

Tia nodded and tried to pull her hand away, but Shane held on. They walked back to camp hand-in-hand.

Everyone stared at them as they crested the hill. Their glances darted from them to the door of Raven's wigwam. Shane's heart thumped madly in his chest. He couldn't imagine what his reaction would be if the big native opened the flap at that very moment. He knew it could potentially get ugly. The prospect of a fight sent a surge of adrenaline through his body, but he wasn't worried; he'd been in more than his fair share of fights in his lifetime. Although he didn't consider himself a tough guy, he'd been known to go from zero to lethal in sixty seconds or less.

He felt the tremor of Tia's body traveling through her arm and into her hand. It grew cold and clammy with her fear. Shane squeezed her hand a little tighter and looked down at her upturned face with a smile. She held his gaze as if drawing strength from him and returned his smile. Shoulders back and head held high she continued on towards the fire with renewed courage. Once there, Shane sat down and Tia busied herself pouring each of them a hot cup of tea. She handed Shane his and set hers down before she disappeared into the wigwam for a second, returning with brush in hand.

Shane looked at her; the corner of his mouth lifted in a smile. He pursed his lips tightly together and nodded consent to the question in her eyes. Tia stood behind Shane's chair and began untangling the snarls from his hair.

"Tell me, what is that soap your mother gave me to use? It smells a little woodsy, spicy even." He closed his eyes and enjoyed having someone brush his hair. Kelly used to sit behind him on the couch for hours watching movies while she brushed his long hair.

"It is my mother's secret recipe. One day, she will pass it on to me. All I know is that she collects juniper berries and grinds them up very fine. After that, she adds oil that she makes from rosewood. It is a lengthy process," she replied, following the path of the brush with her other hand. "Each fall, for at least three days, she has her own fire to make enough soap for everyone. Nobody, not even me, can go near the fire."

Shane chuckled. He pictured Noni guarding her fire like a bear protecting her cubs. For a tiny slip of a woman, she commanded a strong presence—one to be respected if a person had any brains.

"Do you want your hair braided?" Tia asked.

He reached back and slid his hand down the length of his mane. It felt like silk. "No, but maybe later, if you don't mind. I've had my hair tied back for the past week. It feels good to let it hang loose."

Tia sat down next to him and frowned at her empty cup. Taking Shane's, she stepped back to the fire and refilled both cups. Her glance flitted over the camp. Most everyone had gone back to doing their chores. The flap to Raven's wigwam moved, and Tia darted to her seat.

"He's awake," she whispered fearfully.

Shane didn't have to ask whom. Her entire body emanated fear. He took a deep breath and let it out slowly, preparing himself for the inevitable.

From the other direction, a group of men walked towards the camp. Shane saw Gray Owl amongst them. Now maybe they would know exactly how things stood. He noticed Tia's tension as her father approached.

"Relax, Tia," Shane leaned over and whispered in her ear. "You're not alone in this battle. Remember, I'm on your side."

Tia turned to him; her eyes pooled with unshed tears. "Thank you."

Chief separated from the men and walked over to their fire. He looked at ease and his skin had a youthful glow from spending the past two days on the water. He held his hand out towards Shane and stopped in front of him.

"Congratulations," he offered. "We have much to discuss. After we all have some breakfast, I would like to speak to you alone."

Shane held the chief's intense look. He couldn't read his mood, but his expression told him the importance of what he wished to discuss. "Don't you think Tia should be included? It's her future we're deciding."

Chief shook his head. "I will be talking to Raven over breakfast, then we talk. After, we will all sit together."

"I'll be waiting." Shane knew disagreeing with the man wouldn't change a thing. Chief had spoken; end of discussion. What he wouldn't give to be a fly on the wall at his breakfast with Raven.

"Your meal will be brought over to you. I will call you when I am ready for our talk." Gray Owl turned and ducked inside his wigwam.

"I'll bring your breakfast," Tia stammered. She rose from her seat and hurried to begin meal preparations.

Shane exhaled noisily and stood. He set his empty cup down and turned to leave just as Raven approached. The two men stopped and glared at one another. Shane saw the rage seething in the man's eyes. It was obvious that Raven wouldn't tell anyone about the rendezvous at the mud pit.

Fine by me, asshole. We both know the truth. Let's see what kind of a man you really are.

Shane turned on his heel and left Raven standing alone. He crossed the distance to his wigwam. Next to the entrance flap, he sat down on a stump and looked back. Raven remained in the same spot. He snarled at Shane, spat on the ground, and whirled on his heel to join Chief inside his wigwam.

It didn't take long for the women to put together breakfast. Afterwards, Shane sat outside alone. Moving his food around on his plate, his gaze stayed glued to the wigwam's door, where Raven and Chief sat inside. Would the big Indian tell Gray Owl about his part in helping him out of the mud pit? Without his aid, he would've died. Would he throw a fit or accept the chief's decision?

He watched Tia fumble with the breakfast dishes. In her nervousness, she dropped this and that. Her mother finally lost her temper and sent her to fetch some water.

Part of him wanted to follow her, but he needed to be here if Chief called for him. Besides, he needed to see what kind of mood Raven was in when he left from his meeting. Finally, Raven appeared. Shane couldn't tell anything from his expression. He watched him stomp over to his wigwam and disappear inside.

Noni joined her husband and came back out carrying two plates of half-eaten food. Looking in his direction, she nodded for him to enter.

Shane breathed deeply and straightened his shoulders. *Here goes nothing!*

Entering the wigwam, his eyes stung from the tobacco smoke that filled the small space. He hoped the chief didn't expect him to partake of the stuff.

"Come sit by me," Gray Owl said, drawing deeply on his pipe. "You have won the race. Now, Tia will not have to marry Raven—if that is her wish."

Shane breathed a sigh of relief and smiled. "I'm happy to hear that."

"I am not finished. I must ask: do you plan on marrying my daughter?"

An uncomfortable lump rose in his throat. He'd been battling with his answer for some time. Yes, there was an undeniable chemistry between Tia and him, but Kelly had not been gone even a month. For him to consider marrying another woman, even to save her from the likes of Raven, was wrong on so many levels.

"If Tia is able to make her own decision, I feel no need to force her to marry me. It would be no better than making her marry Raven. She is still very much in love with Danti and she knows I am still very much in love with my wife."

Iron Horse Rider

A long, uncomfortable pause followed. Finally, Chief replied, "I had a feeling you would say that." He sighed. "This is Raven's home and if you do not intend to marry Tia, I hope you see this leaves me in a rather difficult position. Raven has agreed he will not cause trouble if the two of you do marry." He paused yet again and puffed on his pipe. "I want you to think long and hard before you answer my question. If you choose to marry her, I welcome you to our family, but if you choose not to marry my daughter, it is with great sadness that I must ask you to leave."

Shane opened his mouth to respond but could find no words.

"I am giving you three days. I ask you to give this a great deal of thought. Talk to Tia, listen to your heart, then we will meet again."

Shane stood, feeling overwhelmed by the entire situation. He hadn't been expecting this outcome. *How could Raven suggest that he leave after saving his life? Was his macho pride really that important to him?* He shook his head sadly and exited the wigwam. *Three days. I have to make a decision in three days. I need to talk to Tia and find out how she feels.*

Shane headed directly for the water. He knew she'd be so happy to be free from marrying Raven, but how would she feel about the rest of it? He stopped in his tracks. *Maybe I should just go. I already know she has no desire to marry me, so why should it bother me so much? Is it possible to love two women at the same time? How can I feel this way so soon after Kelly's death?*

He looked around at the place he'd come to think of as his home. *How can I leave here? I can't go back and live the life I had. Not after living here.*

He turned and strode in the opposite direction. Right now, he needed some time alone. When Tia returned her father would fill her in on what had happened.

How can I consider marrying again when my heart still aches for Kelly? The day I said my vows, I meant them. Until death do us part—she died and I am very much alive. I can't deny my feelings for Tia. If I leave, will I be walking away from my last chance at love?

Chapter Sixteen

Tia heard the men folk returning from their day of fishing. Their voices carried on the wind full of laughter and jesting. Initially, her impulse was to drop the pails and run to find him. Fear kept her staring down at the rippling water.

What if all Shane's hard work was for nothing? I'll never forgive Father if he goes back on his word. Surely he couldn't be so cruel.

After she filled the pails and set them up at the base of the path, she waded out and climbed atop a boulder. The image of Shane's naked body caused a shiver to run up her spine. He was nothing like she had imagined him to be. After she met him that first time, she'd planned to steer clear of the white man with the strange markings on his arms, but that same man had gone above and beyond kindness to help her. How could she ever repay him?

"Tia," shouted Noni from the top of the path. "Your father would like to speak with you now."

Her heart skipped a beat, and she waved to her mother. In a matter of moments, she would know her fate. Her stomach twisted in knots and the sourness traveled up her throat. Bent over, with one hand on the boulder, she vomited. She leaned over, scooped up a handful of clean water, and splashed her face. All of this worry had taken its toll on her. With renewed determination, she picked up the pails and staggered up the path.

At the mouth of the path, Noni hurried over to her. She took the pails and set them down. "What's wrong, Tia?" she asked. "You look like you've been seeing spirits."

"I...I'm fine." Tia looked over at the wigwam where her father waited inside to talk to her. She took a deep breath and straightened. "At least, I hope I'm fine," she added before going over and pushing aside the flap.

Her father sat before the fire, and upon her arrival, set down his pipe. He unfolded his long legs and stood. With a hand on each of her arms he pulled her to him, kissing both her cheeks. "Don't look so afraid, Tia. Thanks to our friend, you are free to do as you choose."

Tia's jaw dropped. "Is this true?" she asked.

Chief chuckled. "Yes, it is true."

Tia smiled and tears rolled down her cheeks. She flung herself at her father, almost knocking him off of his feet.

"Whoa!" He laughed.

"Oh, Father," she cried. "Does this really mean I don't have to marry?" She pressed her hands to her mouth and closed her eyes against the tears escaping through her lashes. "Thank you," she whispered.

"Come sit down with me. There is something more we must discuss."

Tia hiccupped and shuddered. She drew a shaky breath and willed the tears to stop.

***

Now what?

Shane sat under a big, old willow tree; he'd come to think of it as his thinking place. At home, he always sat behind the house in an oversized wooden chair and lost himself in the beauty of the mountains. Now, he reclined against the knotted trunk and watched the paint-worn hulls of fishing boats pass slowly by.

Shane didn't want to leave this place where peace had finally found him. He knew Raven had insisted that he leave. Now, he wouldn't have to worry about everyone finding out he'd saved the man's sorry ass. It meant little to Raven that Tia didn't want to marry him. There were plenty of women to choose from. If it weren't Tia it would be someone else. Being bested by a white man was an entirely different issue. It was a matter of ego and his reputation amongst his people. Little did Raven know there were few who held him in high regard.

Shane had no one but himself to blame for getting into this situation. He shouldn't have been so stupid to open his heart again, especially so soon. When would he learn that in doing so pain would find him? No, he had to save the damsel in distress; he had to save his rival from certain death too.

What did any of these good deeds do for him? *Nothing, absolutely nothing.*

Tia would go on with her life and eventually fall in love and marry again. Raven would find another victim to marry, and Shane would ride off into the sunset, destined to spend his days alone.

This is insane. In three days I'm supposed to decide if I want to force a woman to marry me, or hit the road. Neither option seems like much of a choice to me.

Shane needed to go for a ride and clear his head. Maybe when he returned he'd track down Tia and discuss things. Hell, now that she'd been given her freedom, she'd probably run the other way.

He rose and skirted the camp to his bike. He hoped by taking the long way around he'd avoid running into anyone, especially Raven. Right now, he didn't trust himself not to jump all over the asshole.

Keeping to the tree line that enclosed the village, he moved from one tree to another until he reached the back of a wooden shack and saw Tia coming from her father's wigwam, her eyes red and puffy. She looked totally lost standing there alone. He'd thought she'd be thrilled to hear the news.

With a heavy sigh, he rounded the side of the hut; he had to find out what was wrong. His gaze moved to Raven, who had just crested the top of the path leading from the water. Quickly, he opened the door to the hut and slipped inside. Closing the door behind him, he crouched in the darkness. Without any windows in the structure to allow light inside, he blinked in the darkness and waited for his eyes to adjust. His hand came to rest on something smooth and cool. With his palms flat, he followed the surfaces and planes of the thing, his eyes beginning to see a darker shape looming before him. If he didn't know better, he'd swear it was a motorcycle. Cool metal and the unmistakable shape of handlebars left him puzzled.

What the hell is a bike doing here?

He pushed the door open, and bright sunlight filled the hut. He stood back, staring in disbelief. Over the years, he'd relived the day in his mind many times. There was no mistaking the bike.

What was his father's bike doing here?

He staggered back, nearly falling on his ass, his hands shaking uncontrollably. Out of the corner of his eye, he saw one of the village men point in his direction and heard him call out for someone to get the chief. By the time Gray Owl made his way over to Shane, a small crowd had gathered around him. Shane stared at the bike, his mouth agape.

Chief reached over and touched Shane's shoulder. He whirled around angrily, and the chief pulled his hand back.

"Please, Shane. You must let me explain. Come with me. We'll have some tea and talk."

"Talk?" snarled Shane. "Have some fucking tea and talk? How about I ask the questions, and you give the answers?" Rage flowed through him like a black storm cloud.

"What is my father's bike doing here?"

Chief shifted uncomfortably from one foot to the other. He cleared his throat and replied, "It is a long story. I think it is best if we talk alone." He reached out to Shane.

He shrugged off the older man as if his slightest touch would sear his flesh. "You better talk fast, old man, I only have *three* days. Remember?"

Chief shook his head and took a deep breath. "Your father used to come here often. He always talked about you."

"Came *here*? Why would he come here?" asked Shane in disbelief.

"To visit his mother." Chief kept his head bowed as he spoke. Tia moved to his side and held his arm in support.

Shane looked from him to Tia. "Did you know about this?"

Tears trickled from her eyes, and with her head bowed, she nodded.

"Great! Just fucking wonderful. *If* this is true, where is my father—and my grandmother?" With clenched fists, he struggled to reign in his anger.

"Your father died while out fishing. He loved the water, but after he married, he didn't come visit as often. One afternoon, he jumped in for a swim and the undercurrent took him down." Chief stopped to clear his throat and dab at his eyes with the edge of his sleeve. "We tried to help but the current was too strong."

"If you knew about me, why didn't you call us when it happened?" Angry tears ran unchecked down his face.

"We knew of your mother's hatred of us. Why do you think he never brought you here? Your mother made him promise to never show you this half of your heritage. If he broke his word, she would take you far away." Anger and disappointment laced his words.

Disgusted, Shane shook his head. He hadn't seen his mother in more than thirty years. Not since the day he'd left home. After all this time, she'd still managed to fuck up his life.

"We did tell your mother. I will not repeat what she said, but I didn't know she'd never told you about your father's death." Briefly, Chief looked Shane in the eyes. "Until you rode into camp the other day, I'd never laid eyes on you. It wasn't until I saw the bell that I knew who you were."

Shane staggered back. *Oh, fuck! Don't be telling me this.* He closed his eyes and braced himself to hear what he already suspected.

"Surely by now you know the spirit that has been helping you is your father."

Shane lifted his head and looked straight in the chief's glistening amber eyes. "Are you telling me the strange biker I've been seeing is my father?" He took a deep breath and held it, his gaze still locked with the Chief's.

"Yes."

Somehow, he realized he'd sensed it the entire time, but chose to ignore the whispers of his mind and heart. Ever since the accident, there had been something so familiar about him. Oddly enough, he'd never freaked when the...when his father's ghost had shown up. He'd just accepted it. The chief *and* Tia had both known.

Shane looked around at all the silent faces staring back at him. "I bet all of you knew," he yelled. Trembling and pacing back and forth, he ran his hands through his hair and let out a low whistle. "This is just too much to wrap my brain around. I'm outta here."

Shane brushed Gray Owl's hand aside as he hurried off towards his bike. Frantic to escape, he half ran, half jogged across the camp. With the heel of one hand, he wiped the tears from his eyes and sniffed. He straddled Belle, tuning out the villagers coming toward him. He kicked her to life and spun the bike around to face the laneway. Without so much as a glance back, he twisted the wick and sped away from camp.

Shane had no idea where he was going, but he knew he needed to distance himself from everything. How many times had he seen the same blue fender riding away from him in his dreams? It never crossed his mind that he couldn't come back, that his mother was the one responsible for everything.

Now it all made sense. His father had died, and his mother had known the whole time. Rage gurgled in the pit of his stomach. Never had he hated her as much as he hated her at that very moment. No wonder her best friend was a bottle of Jack Daniels.

He tilted his head back and bellowed laughter that bordered on hysteria. *My whole life has been a fucking lie!*

The only good and honest things in his life were dead. First, his father, and then Kelly. He stared at the road through a blur of tears. *Never again will I let anyone in my heart.* He shuddered, thinking how close he'd come to letting Tia in. It didn't mean he loved Kelly any less—he would always love her.

Why wouldn't they have told him about his father? None of it made any sense. Even his father appearing here and there didn't add up. He could have told him right from the beginning. Shane remembered the strange words of Chief White Wolf, *"If you ever find yourself in trouble, all you need to do is ring the bell and he will come."*

Not fucking likely. It'll be a cold day in hell when I ring anybody's bell!

Shane's tire grabbed the gravel shoulder. The front wheel wobbled, jarring his attention back to the road. He struggled to keep the bike steady. Looking around, Shane had no idea where he was until he saw the familiar gas bar where he and Tia had stopped during their ride. The spot behind it made the perfect hiding place and there would be less chance of him killing himself on his bike. Shane turned into the small lot, riding slowly by the front door. A sign taped to the glass pane read: Gone Fishing.

Perfect. He'd ride his bike out back so no one saw him from the road. He pulled Belle up behind the building. Mud splashed up and covered his boots, the ground still soft from the heavy rain. Finding a flat piece of stone, he put it under the kickstand.

He remembered the half bottle of shine in his saddlebag. "Fuck it," he growled and opened his saddlebag to dig out the bottle. He'd worry about the hangover later.

As he trudged through the mud to the high-backed chairs, Shane unscrewed the cap. He tipped the bottle and swallowed deeply. He sputtered and coughed, the clear liquid blazing a trail down his throat. A fiery explosion erupted in the pit of his stomach.

"Whoooeeee!" He wiped his mouth on his shirtsleeve. Sitting down in the chair, a promising numbness tingled through his body, and the hair on the back of his neck stood on end.

Chapter Seventeen

"Father, you have to send someone to find him," Tia begged shortly after Shane left.

Her father walked directly to the big meeting place. He sat smoking his pipe, staring off in space, a look of deep sadness etched on his face. "Where would we look Tia? He is long gone by now."

Tia knelt beside her father. Tears streamed down her face, and her heart ached like it would break into a million pieces. The way Shane had looked at her had chilled her to the very core. She didn't blame him for being angry. They should have told him the first day he arrived at the camp, but they kept their promise. Shane's father wanted to be the one to tell him and they had vowed to let him do it in his own time.

"Do you think he will come back, father?" She sniffed.

"I think once he has calmed down he might." Gray Owl reached up and pushed her sodden hair from her face. "Even if it's just to give us a piece of his mind before he leaves us for good." He bowed his head and closed his eyes. "We must pray he gives us the opportunity to explain."

Tia curled up next to her father and laid her head against his chest. "I love him," she confessed. "I don't know when it happened, Father. I miss Danti so much it hurts sometimes, but I love Shane. If he decides not to come back..." She dissolved into tears.

His embrace tightened around her and he began praying softly into her hair.

* * *

Shane tilted the bottle back and drained the last of its contents. Tossing the empty bottle on the ground beside him, he cocked his head to one side and listened. The distant rumble of a motorcycle reached him.

"Oh, no." He shook his head vigorously from side to side. "No, you don't."

He tried to lift himself from the chair, but lost his grip on the wide arms. He fell back onto it, smacking his head on the back.

"Shit!"

The rumble grew louder.

Shane just wanted to disappear. He managed to get to his feet, swaying back and forth, his head spinning. He reached behind him and lowered himself back down. *Not such a good idea.* He held his head in his hands and moaned.

A cool breeze feathered across the back of his neck. He looked up to see his father. He sat on his bright blue Indian; this time, the setting sun shone through him and the bike.

"Hey, daddio! Where the hell have you been all my life?" Shane slurred sarcastically.

"I'm here now," his father said with conviction. "You left behind several people who are pretty worried about you right now."

Shane laughed. "Yah? And who might they be? Chief? Tia? Or maybe Raven is all broken up about it."

"You left before they had a chance to explain. They wanted to tell you the truth, but I asked them not to, so if you need to blame someone, blame me."

Shane eyed the apparition that sat before him. Even through blurred vision, he knew it was his father. He looked a little older than the last time he saw him, his long hair gray around the temples.

"Why did you wait so long to show yourself for who you really are, or that you're a...a ghost? And don't tell me any more lies! I've been told enough lies to last a lifetime."

"Nobody wanted to lie to you. After I died, the only ones who saw me were those who were open to the possibility. You see, until you knew the truth, I had to keep my identity from you."

"Bullshit! It's all a bunch of bullshit!" Shane lurched to his feet. He held the back of the chair and stumbled around it.

"You've had too much to drink. I don't think it's wise for you to get on your bike right now."

Shane erupted in a fit of laughter, stopping in his tracks. He glared at his father, trying desperately to catch his breath. "*Now* you want to be my father? Now you think you can just up and tell me what to do?" He swaggered towards his bike, his feet sliding in the mud. Losing his balance, he reached out to his bike to catch himself. The bike teetered under his weight. The stone under the kickstand disappeared in the mud. Shane fell flat on his ass.

"Damn!" He shook the mud from his hands. The trace of a smile he saw on his father's face pissed him off even more. "I don't need you! I don't need anybody! Why don't you just saddle up and go wherever dead people are supposed to go?"

He tried to right himself but only managed to sink further in the mud. The more he moved, the harder it became to lift his hands from the muck. Shane wasn't the only thing sinking. His bike was buried up to the floorboards, and every time he tried to push himself out, it sank further.

Shane wasn't so drunk he couldn't see he needed help. Now he understood how helpless Raven must have felt trapped in the mud pit.

He looked over at the empty space where his father had stood. Shane looked around. The sun descended on the horizon, and the twilight made it difficult to see. *He left me again. That lying son of a bitch left me again.* He looked down at himself, his body a mud-soaked mess. Next to him, Belle lay firmly stuck in the mire. Looking up at the sky, he screamed. "Help! Will somebody please help me!" *You sorry-assed loser. Look at the mess you've gotten yourself into now.*

* * *

Darkness blanketed the mountains. Worry sickened Tia. She couldn't begin to imagine how Shane must feel. She wouldn't blame him if he never wanted to see any of them again. She just wanted to know that he was okay. Tia sat staring into the fire. The breeze whispering against her face drew her attention. She turned towards it and saw Shane's father sitting next to her. She'd seen him before but it startled her just the same.

"Shane needs your help," Sam said, his face creased with concern. "You need to persuade Raven to go help him."

Tia stared at him in disbelief, her heart pounding fiercely. "Raven? What could possibly make Raven think he should help him?" She jumped to her feet, her eyes wide with panic. "Where is Shane? I will go."

"No, there is nothing you can do. Raven owes Shane, so he will go."

"I don't understand," she said, her eyes brimming with tears. "What does Raven owe Shane?"

"I want you to remind Raven he owes Shane for saving his life."

"His life? Is that true?" Tia stared at him in disbelief.

"You must hurry. If Raven does not listen to you, then you must have your father talk to him."

"Does my father know how Shane saved Raven's life?"

"No, but I will tell him while you are gone. Tell Raven that Shane is behind Billy's store. He knows where it is."

Tia's mind raced. Billy's store? Could it be the same place where they stopped the other day?

"Go now," Sam ordered.

Tia ran to Raven's wigwam. She glanced back at the fire, but Shane's father had disappeared. "Raven! Raven, you must wake up!"

Raven sat up in bed and rubbed his eyes. "What? Tia? Is that you?"

"You have to get up. Shane's in trouble and he needs you to go to him now. Hurry!" Her words burst out, her breathing ragged.

"Why would I want to help him?" he asked.

"Because he saved your life." Her voice cracked. "Now, he needs you."

Raven snickered. "You're out of your mind." He lay back down and pulled a skin over his head.

Panic seized Tia. "You must get up. You either get up for me, or I will go for my father."

The words had barely left her lips, and her father appeared in the doorway. "I think you need to listen to my daughter," he said. "I know what happened on your way to White Wolf's camp. I know how Shane saved your life."

Raven jerked up from bed, looking none too pleased. "I don't know where you two have been getting your information, but you are both mistaken. The white man did not save my life."

Chief Gray Owl looked Raven straight in the eye. "Look me in the eyes, Raven, and tell me he did not save your life."

Raven looked down and sighed heavily. "Where is he?"

"He's behind Billy's store. You must hurry!" Tia reached for a shirt that lay crumpled on the ground and tossed it at him.

Chief reached in his pocket and pulled out a set of keys, throwing them at Raven. "Take the truck. Now go!"

Raven's eyes flashed with anger as he caught the keys in mid air. He looked from one to the other and left the wigwam in a huff.

"Make sure you take some rope!" Chief shouted behind him.

Raven kept on walking and waved his hand in the air. On the brink of hysteria, Tia stared at her father. He met her eyes and nodded his head. She tore off after Raven. If she'd had to stay and wait, she would've gone mad.

"I'm going with you," she cried, trying to catch her breath.

"You're crazy. I don't need your help," he barked at her and quickened his pace.

"I didn't ask you, I'm *telling* you."

Raven shrugged and reached for the truck's door handle. "Suit yourself, but stay out of the way."

Tia jumped in the back of the truck. No way could she sit next to the man. Holding on to the sides of the box, she braced herself for a rough ride. Given how angry Raven was, he certainly wouldn't be making the trip an easy one for her.

He started the engine with a roar and cranked the wheel hard before he stepped on the gas.

It took every ounce of her strength to hold on. *Bastard!* she thought, bouncing up and down in the back as he guided the truck away from camp. Her hair whipped around in the wind, pelting her face. She wondered what kind of trouble had befallen Shane. Tia couldn't figure out why he never mentioned any incident between him and Raven. Of course, he wouldn't, he's too much of a man. For the remainder of the ride, she prayed to Glooscap to keep Shane safe until they could get to him.

Without warning, the truck screeched and turned hard. Tia lost hold of one side and crashed into the sidewall of the box. The truck jolted to a stop. Stunned, she lay still for a moment. Slowly, she moved, fearful her arm might be broken. It hurt like hell but she could move it. Wincing from the pain, she stood up in the box and leaned against the back window.

The only light came from the moon reflecting off the water. "Turn on your lights!" She called. "It's too dark!"

The lights of the truck flared to life, and Raven climbed out of the truck. Tia jumped down from the back. The glint off the chrome on his bike caught her attention before she saw him. Raven stood with his arms folded, laughing out loud.

Tia looked down at Shane. He lay stretched out in a pit of mud, his mouth wide open and snoring loudly. His bike sat in mud up to its tire rims. If it hadn't been for how loud he snored, Tia would have thought him dead. Given his predicament, she couldn't help but grin too. The overwhelming stench of moonshine reached her.

She asked, "How are we going to get him out of that mess?"

Raven shook his head, still laughing. "I guess we tie a rope around the bike and pull it out." He laughed harder. "We might have to do the same with him too."

Tia climbed up the tailgate and pulled the rope from the back of the truck. "What do you want me to do?"

Raven grabbed the rope from her and frowned. "Stay out of my way. If I need your help, I'll ask."

Tia pouted and crossed her arms. She watched Raven carefully wade through the muck. He threaded a rope around the frame. He eased over to the side of the bike and hiked a long leg over the seat.

"Get in the truck. Wait until I say go before you pull ahead nice and slowly." Raven barked the order.

Ignoring his gruffness, Tia ran to the driver's door and yanked it open. She hopped behind the steering wheel, turned the key in the ignition, and stuck her head out the door. "Now?"

Raven waved her on. He put both hands firmly on the grips and guided the bike out of the mud. Tia looked back to make sure the bike sat on stable ground. Satisfied, she gave the old truck some gas, jarring Raven enough that he fell off the bike and into the mud.

Tia stayed in the truck until she thought she could face Raven without laughing. She turned off the truck and ran back to see Raven struggling to get up. He breathed heavily as he wiped at his face in a futile attempt to remove the mud.

"Oops," she said sweetly and batted her eyelashes.

"I bet." He righted the bike and put it on its stand. "Think you can watch that it doesn't start sinking again?"

Tia nodded, not trusting herself to speak. It took every ounce of restraint not to dissolve into a fit of laughter.

Raven stood back seemingly assessing the situation before he planted his feet firmly on either side of Shane's body. Reaching down, he grabbed him under the arms and pulled with all his might. Tia heard the mud sucking at Shane's body as he slowly came free. Suddenly Raven went flying back. The weight of Shane crashed down on top of him.

"Oh my!" Tia shrieked with laughter, unable to hold back any longer. Raven lay flat on his back, Shane on top of him, still snoring loudly. Tia wondered how much he must have drunk to be able to sleep through all this.

"Are you just going to stand there all night laughing, or are you going to give me a hand?" Raven asked through clenched teeth.

Tia pulled Shane up enough that Raven could roll away. He looked down at Shane while attempting to catch his breath.

"Asshole." He stepped over him to tend to the bike.

Raven set the wood they used to load their boats against the tailgate. The mud covered bike resisted, but he managed to maneuver it up the ramp. Once in the box, he tied it down with the rope. He stood bent over with his hands on his thighs, trying to catch his breath. It took him a few minutes before he straightened and looked at Tia.

"I'll take him under his arms and you get his feet. We'll have to put him in the front with me." He frowned. "Ready?"

Tia nodded and grabbed Shane's ankles. She struggled, using all of her strength as they hoisted him up and wrangled him onto the seat. He curled up in a fetal position and resumed his loud snoring.

Raven took one look at Shane and shook his head. "On second thought, you will drive home." Raven jumped up in the back of the truck. He sat on the wheel well and braced his feet on the side of the bike. "Take it easy on the turns so the bike doesn't fall over."

Tia nodded and ran over to the driver's door. She climbed behind the wheel and pulled out onto the road. In the mirror, she saw Raven sitting on the side of the truck, covered head to toe in mud, his expression one of immense anger. No matter what she thought of him, he did get Shane out of one hell of a mess. She didn't know what Shane had done to save his life, but hoped they were even now.

At camp, the second she put the truck in park, Raven jumped out and stormed off toward the water. Her father jogged over with her mother close behind him. He looked in the passenger window and opened the door.

"Is he okay?" Chief asked, scrunching up his nose at the stench that assaulted him. "He's drunk?"

Tia nodded. "He never woke up once." She giggled. "Father, you had to be there to understand."

Confusion creased his brow and he stared oddly at his daughter. "This is funny?" he asked.

Tia laughed harder. "I will tell you after we get him to bed."

"We need to clean him up before we put him in bed," Noni stated, looking in on the snoring mud pile. "Carry him over by the fire. I have some water in pails sitting outside."

"He's pretty heavy," said Tia.

"We will leave him right where he is," said Chief. "He will be okay here. Take the keys for the truck and his bike so he can't run off."

"But father," said Tia.

"No buts." He waved his hand at her. "Bring a blanket out to him if you like. He will be fine where he is."

Tia knew from her father's tone not to argue. Even though she wasn't happy about it, she knew he was right. She watched her parents head off to bed and she fetched a couple skins from around the fire. Tia tucked the skins over Shane's sleeping body. The smell coming from him made her eyes water and her stomach churn. Why anyone would drink that much shine was beyond her comprehension.

Once she was convinced he'd be warm, she closed the door of the truck. Tia stood looking in the window at his sleeping face. Would this man ever be able to forgive her for keeping the truth from him? Come morning, he would wake up feeling badly. She would make sure she had plenty of sarsaparilla tea ready for him. It would make his head stop pounding and then maybe he would talk to her. There had to be a way to make him see her side of things.

Tia walked slowly back to the fire. She saw a long night ahead of her. She sat down and pulled a skin around her shoulders. Sleep would not come to her tonight; this she knew for certain. She would pray to the powers that be for Shane to find it in his heart to forgive her. After Danti died, she swore there would never be another man in her life. She was wrong; what she felt for Shane didn't compare to how she felt for Danti. It was love nonetheless. How could she make him see? Did she dare hope he might feel the same way?

Tears trickled down her cheeks as she stared at the truck parked across the way.

Chapter Eighteen

Shane hurt from the top of his head down to his toes. He lay with his eyes closed, trying to collect his thoughts. He remembered talking to his father.

The mud. He remembered the mud.

Slowly he opened his eyes, his head screaming in protest. He focused on the space in front of him. A dashboard? He turned his head. Shooting pain traveled from behind his eyes to the top of his skull. He tasted the sour staleness of the moonshine he'd drunk. He groaned and closed his eyes.

How did I get here? He tried desperately to remember something, anything. The last thing he recalled was seeing his father, followed by falling in the mud. *Did my father bring me here? Where am I?* With extreme caution, he slowly moved into a sitting position. Once his head stopped spinning, he opened his eyes a crack. He saw the familiar outline of wigwams back at the camp. Bit by bit, he remembered the details of the night before.

They'd all known about his father, yet not one of them had told him the truth. If he hadn't stumbled upon his motorcycle, would they ever have told him? He scanned the village. It seemed everyone slept. The sun had just begun to rise; a pink glow illuminated everything. Shane saw someone huddled in front of a fire.

He turned his head and looked out the back window. In the pickup bed, completely splattered with mud, sat his bike. Who had brought him back? It wouldn't have been an easy task putting his bike in the back of the truck. Movement caught his attention. The figure at the fire stirred. The skin around the person fell, and he saw Tia.

There is no way in hell she put the bike in this truck on her own.

The thick layer of mud covering him had begun to harden. If he didn't get out of his clothes soon, he'd turn into a statue. With great care, he mindfully edged across the seat to the door. He rubbed his muddy hands together, shaking loose the caked mud and inched open the door. Shane didn't feel up to talking to anyone right now and willed Tia not to wake up.

If I can just make it down to the water. With his body a quivering mass of pain, worry and uncertainty, he grabbed one of the skins off the truck seat and wrapped it around himself. It took quite some time before he made it down the path. His jeans had dried stiffly, so bending his knees became quite a task. If he'd been thinking straight, he should have taken them off at the truck.

Iron Horse Rider

At the water's edge, he fell to the ground, every ounce of his strength spent. He knew he needed to get out of his clothes but lacked the energy to do so. Stretched out on the sand, he closed his eyes, his mind a jumble of events that led him to this very place in time.

* * *

Tia watched through narrow slits as Shane struggled his way to the trail. He needed this time to recoup and she wasn't in any hurry to find out how much he hated her. Holding her breath for fear she'd move and give herself away, Tia sat motionless. Only after he disappeared from her sight did she dare release it.

Standing, she painfully stretched her body. It looked like Shane would be in desperate need of coffee this morning. Tia busied herself making a fresh pot. Once it sat on the grate over a rekindled fire, she sat down heavily. Slowly, the place she called home began showing signs of life. She wondered how the future would unfold. Would Shane really leave them or could he find it in his heart to forgive?

Tia heard a noise behind her and turned to see her mother coming out of their wigwam. The dark circles under her eyes told of yet another person who had nearly no sleep. Tia forced a smile, hoping she wouldn't start questioning her just yet.

Noni walked over to her daughter and stroked her hair. "It looks like the men weren't the only ones playing in the mud yesterday."

Tia gasped, opening up the skin she'd wrapped around her. "Oh, dear. I better change." Standing again, she tossed the skin aside. Before she could move, she tugged on her dress.

"You might want to wash your face while you're at it." Noni grinned.

Tia groaned and hurried out behind their wigwam to a basin of wash water. After she'd scrubbed her face, she looked down at the once clear water, the basin now a muddy pool. She tossed the water a little ways back from the wigwam and started walking toward the path with the empty basin. Stopping in her tracks, embarrassment heated her cheeks.

The last time she'd seen Shane down by the water, she'd caught him in a rather compromising position. Her heart beat rapidly at the memory. On second thought, she'd wait until he returned. Quickly, she put the basin back and crept inside the wigwam where she changed into a fresh dress of tanned deerskin. On her feet, she wore knee high moccasins, beautifully decorated with beaded fringes.

The smell of fresh coffee wafted inside the wigwam. She looked over at her sleeping father, amused at his nose wriggling in his sleep. He'd soon be awake. Tia picked up a basket filled with her brush and hair ornaments. Maybe she could persuade her mother to fix her hair.

Fortunately, Tia didn't even have to ask. Noni handed her a mug of hot coffee the second she stepped outside. "Sit down," she instructed before taking the basket from her.

"Thank you." Tia smiled. She sat down, her gaze lingering on the mouth of the path. "Do you think he will stay?"

Noni sighed wearily. "I do not know, child." Her fingers worked to remove the mud covered braids from her daughter's hair. "He has every reason to be angry at us, his father, and his God. Let's hope he will listen to us before making any more decisions in anger."

Tia nodded in agreement, her heart aching. "I love him," she whispered.

"I can see this," she soothed. "His heart is not open to love, Tia. He is still very much in love with his wife. Do not mistake his kindness for something more."

Tears stung Tia's eyes. Her voice quivered as she spoke. "Maybe so, but it does not change how I feel. What am I to do, Mother?"

Noni began easing the brush through Tia's mass of tangles; the drying mud fell to the ground with every stroke. "Be patient. Trust that things will unfold as they are meant to."

"Listen to your mother," spoke Chief Gray Owl. He immerged from the wigwam and joined them.

Noni handed the brush to Tia and scurried over to fetch her husband some coffee. Tia resumed brushing. She knew they were right. The decision wasn't hers to make.

"Where is Shane now?" Gray Owl asked, taking the cup from his wife and sitting down.

* * *

Shane felt *his* presence nudging him awake. Before he opened his eyes, he knew his father had come to him. Slowly, he crept into wakefulness, trying to ready himself for the meeting. Corporeal this time, his father sat next to him, staring out across the water, so close he could reach out and touch him. Rather than be the first to speak, Shane awkwardly sat up in silence and began the monumental task of removing his boots.

The morning sun had all but dried the mud. It cracked and crumbled, falling away as he undressed. Shivering in his boxers, he inched away from shore. Shane braced himself before lunging into the water.

The warmth coursing over the length of his body eased his muscles. He stayed under until his lungs screamed for release. Part of him wanted his father to be gone when he surfaced. Shane knew if he hoped to find any peace of mind, he needed to confront him. There were so many questions that needed answers, but it would be so much simpler just to hop on his bike and ride.

The invigorating water gave him renewed energy. With an intense determination, he swam back to shore. His father still sat waiting for him. A mixture of emotions simmered inside Shane's heart. Avoiding his father's eyes, he shook out the skin he'd taken from the truck. After he wrapped himself in its warmth, he sat down next to his father.

"I'm happy you decided to stay." He spoke with sincerity and conviction and turned to face Shane.

"I don't want to hear any lame excuses. I just need you to answer a few questions," Shane said without looking at him. He tried to absorb the calmness of the ocean sprawled out before them.

"I guess I owe you that much."

Shane's heart wrenched at the sadness he heard in his voice. His resolve weakened and his voice wavered. "Why did you wait so long to show yourself? I don't want to hear any poetic bullshit about my heart being closed either," snapped Shane.

His father expelled a long breath. "It's true. There's no other way to explain it. I've been waiting many years until I could come to you, and now, I will not be able to rest in peace until I know you will be okay."

"You could have come long before the accident."

Sam shook his head. "Up until that day, I never heard you call out for help. I don't know why, but until then, I couldn't make you see me. You have to know how much I love you. I wanted desperately to come long before this."

"I don't know..." Shane buried his face in his hands. "I don't know what to believe anymore."

"Listen to your heart and try not to be too quick to judge others. The people here genuinely care about you. They are my people and now they are yours. Remember, Shane, I did not choose to leave you. You're my son, and I will love you until the end of time."

A warm breeze lifted Shane's wet hair. He knew before looking that his father would be gone.

"I love you too," he whispered to the empty space beside him. If his mother had told him his father died all those years ago, how different would his life have been now? With calm resignation, he stood and walked up the path wearing only his boxers under the skin. He was extra careful not to step on rocks with his bare feet. He'd come back and get his things later.

As the camp came into view, he wasn't surprised to see Tia and her parents watching his every move. Rather than face them, he turned towards his wigwam. His heart pained at the disappointment he saw in Tia's eyes.

Shane took his time dressing and mulled over his options. He knew in his heart what he needed to do, but how? His father's words played over and over in his mind: *these people are your family*. He gathered up his belongings before heading outside and walked directly over to his bike. Someone had unloaded it from the pickup bed. It sat a few feet away, glistening from a fresh washing.

After he put his things in his saddlebags, he turned towards Tia and her parents. The closer he approached their fire, the thicker his nervous tension grew.

Chief Gray Owl opened his mouth to speak, but Shane held up one hand to silence him. "I'll talk. You will listen," he said, his tone softening as he looked from one to the other. "Please." Shane sat on a stump facing them. "I need to leave for a while." Inwardly, he winced at the alarm in each of their eyes. "Please understand I don't hold any ill feelings toward any of you. I just have a lot of things to sort out for myself. It's important to me to know that I will be welcome to return. My father has made me realize that you are all my family."

He looked straight into Chief's eyes and waited for his response.

"Yes, you will always be welcome here. I was wrong to ask you to leave and I am sorry."

"Thank you." Shane smiled, lowering his gaze for a moment. Finally, he looked directly at Tia. Her lower lip trembled and her eyes filled with unshed tears. He knew with certainty that what he was about to ask her was the right decision. Gently, he said, "I want you to come with me."

Tia's mouth fell open and she looked to her parents and back to Shane.

He took her hands in his. In the short time he'd known her, she'd taken up residence in his heart. They both needed time to grieve and possibly explore the possibilities of something more. "You know that I love my wife with all of my heart, but I want to show you there is a life beyond what you have known amongst your family. I'm not making any promises other than I will keep you safe and bring you back here one day."

The tears that filled her eyes spilled over.

Shane saw she was torn between her family and wanting to go with him. He turned back to face Chief Gray Owl. "You have magic in plants and herbs. My magic lies in the wind. I promise to keep her safe and bring her back a more happy and healed woman. Do I have your permission to take Tia with me?"

Chief sighed. "What you ask of me is highly unusual." He reached over and held his wife's hand. "If this is what Tia wants, we will not stand in her way."

Tia jumped up and wrapped her arms around her father to sob against his chest.

"You promise to bring her back to us?" Noni looked at Shane, her eyes full of worry.

Shane smiled and patted her hand. "I promise." He touched Tia's back. "I'd like to leave soon, Tia. There's a whole world out there to see."

Noni stood, taking her daughter's hand. "Let's go and get you packed."

"Pack light." Shane chuckled. "There's not a whole lot of room for luggage on the bike."

He excused himself and ambled over to Belle. He gave her a thorough once over to make sure she was ready to go. He topped off the oil, making a mental note to pick up some more.

Chief Gray Owl approached with two beautiful white skins draped over his arm. "Can you make room for these?" he asked. "They will come in handy on a cool night."

"I think so." Shane smiled. He'd made the right decision to leave. He needed the wind in his face like a junkie needs his next fix. Riding was a part of who he was. He wanted to share the wind's magic with Tia, and maybe one day, after his heart began to heal, they would come back to this place together.

Tia ran across camp towards them. She'd exchanged her long skirt for blue jeans tucked into her knee-high deerskin boots. Shane smiled appreciatively at how the modern clothing hugged her slender curves. Excitement danced in her eyes. She carried a small bundle of clothing and another small bag in her hands. Shane had taken the sleeping bag off the handlebars and rolled the two skins inside it for protection. The roll was bigger than he would've liked, but he knew they'd be happy to have them on cool nights by a crackling fire.

Once he had all of their things secured on Belle, he turned to the chief, offering him his hand.

Gray Owl smiled broadly and pulled him forward in a warm embrace. "Take good care of my girl," he whispered hoarsely in his ear.

Elder Kaya scurried over to them; a stick of burning sweetgrass in her hand left a trail of smoke in her wake. She looked at Chief and he nodded.

She proceeded to circle Shane's bike while she chanted in their native tongue. Kaya feathered the smoke over every inch of iron and chrome. Once she seemed satisfied, she stood before Tia and Shane and continued the ritual. Shane took his cue from Tia and swooped the smoke up and down his body.

Kaya took hold of Tia's hand, her eyes filled with moisture. "I know our Danti is no longer with us, but you will always be a daughter to me. I think he is smiling today."

Kaya moved over to stand in front of Shane. Her weathered hand cupped his face. "Bring her home to us one day soon."

Shane nodded and stooped over, brushing her cheek with his lips. "I will."

Kaya smiled and left to join a group of natives looking on. Everyone bid them an emotional farewell. Shane brought his iron beast to life, and Tia squealed in delight, clapping her hands before putting on her helmet. With one last hug for her parents, she climbed on behind Shane and held on tight.

"We'll be back before the snow falls. Make sure you practice on my father's bike." Shane shouted over his shoulder to Chief. Gray Owl's eyes grew big and he smiled broadly.

Shane gave Belle some gas and guided the Shovelhead down the lane leading from Tia's home. He saw her expression in his mirror. Watching her parents wave good-bye, her lip trembled and her eyes filled with sadness and fear for the unknown. Within minutes of turning onto the main road, her expression changed to one of awe and wonderment as she took in the magnificent view.

Shane looked toward the horizon, his bike hugging the curves as if it had a mind of its own. He knew this had been the right decision for both of them. He didn't know what the future held any more than the next person did; however, he did know the wind caressing his skin had begun to work its usual magic. The sun shone brighter, and his heart filled with happiness. He took comfort in knowing the truth of the bell that hung from the swing arm.

Shane patted Tia's leg with one hand and twisted the throttle with the other, their laughter melding with the thunder of his ironhorse.

Excerpt from

Soul Haven

by

Sonja Baines

Available at

Wild Child Publishing.com

Soul Haven

Kale jolted back to consciousness, tensing to run until pain flooded his nerves and he remembered where he was. The heat was probably fever—not that he could do anything about it even if he wanted to. Maybe he would end up fulfilling Brady's wishes and die in this cell.

Pull yourself together, Tyrell. Kale forced his eyes open and tentatively moved a hand. It seemed attached at least, but he didn't even want to speculate about the condition of his ribs, or his shoulders, or the kneecap that felt filled with boiling water and shattered glass. He was pretty sure it wasn't broken, but it hurt like hell. At least they hadn't hit his head too hard this time.

Gritting his teeth, Kale tried to move to the bed. He managed to rise to hands and knees, but a coughing fit sent him sprawling again. When it was over, he counted a full minute and tried again. This time, he gained his feet and staggered to the bed. He sensed the lady cop behind the desk watching him, probably with disgust. She'd no doubt been filled in on the nature of his supposed crime.

Let her hate me, he thought as he stretched his battered body along the bunk. *Why not? Everyone else does.* Kale preferred the anonymity that came along with the hatred; it kept people from asking questions he didn't want to answer.

Arranging his limbs as best he could to minimize the pain, he closed his eyes and willed himself to sleep. Slumber refused to cooperate, and when he opened them again, it was to see the woman standing in front of the cell door, staring at him.

He stared back, trying not to notice how much better the dark blue uniform looked on her than it did on Brady and Desmond. A few wisps of auburn hair framed her face, and something resembling concern lurked in her hazel eyes. Still, she didn't move, and just when he started to think she was actually a cardboard cutout put up to fill some hiring quota, she whispered, "Did you really kill a cop?"

Kale sighed. He didn't want to talk to her. The best way to ensure this was to confirm her suspicions. "Yes."

Her features hardened, and the accusation in her eyes stirred something in him. When she turned away, he added, "I also shot John Lennon. And Kennedy."

He regretted his sarcasm when she looked at him again and he caught a whiff of sympathy. Damn it. Why couldn't he have kept his mouth shut? Now would come the questions, and the empty expressions of pity if he told the truth—or the loathing, if he related what the rest of the world believed.

But the woman just watched him, and after a minute she said, "We have a first aid kit out here. Why don't I come in there and clean you up a little?"

Kale propped himself up on his elbows. "Are you insane, lady? Your buddies will crucify you if they catch you in here with me."

"All right. Fine." Shrugging, she started back for the desk, but not before he noticed the sting his rejection had caused. Maybe she was just trying to be professional.

He sat up and maneuvered his legs over the side of the bed. "I could use a drink," he said hesitantly.

At first he thought she'd gone back to ignoring him, but she disappeared through a door and came back holding a small paper cup. Reaching the bars, she held it just beyond them and said, "You'll have to come and take it. I'm not allowed to hold it any further in without restraining you."

With a rusty laugh, Kale rose to his feet. "And you were going to just walk right in here to clean me up?" He wobbled four steps, but before he reached her, his knee gave out. He stumbled into the bars and collapsed in a heap on the floor. The cop jerked back, sloshing the water all over him.

"Jesus!" She clutched the cup to her chest. "I'm sorry. Let me get you some more. Can you get up?"

"What are you going to do if I say no? Ask again real nice?" Grimacing, Kale braced his body against the cell bars and pushed up with his feet to gain a few inches. "I'll manage," he said through clenched teeth. "Forget the water."

Her face flushed bright pink, but Kale barely noticed. *Better this way*, he thought. *She'll ask about it. They always do. Easier to hate me...*

Refusing to meet her eyes again, he crawled back onto the bunk and drifted toward sleep, but some part of him remained aware of everything that happened around him—including the way she glared at him, as though he were Hitler incarnate.

That's right. Hate me.

***

Ren didn't like the feelings the man in the hold evoked from her. She shouldn't permit emotions while on duty. They interfered with the job. But in one night, this vagrant managed to put her through an incredible range, from furious to sympathetic, to almost caring—and then right back to furious. Now, against her will, she edged toward pity. She had to get control of herself and start thinking like a cop.

It was three in the morning. Four hours until her shift ended. Four hours until she could start to forget him and the way she'd felt when she'd believed him momentarily innocent. She glanced over at the cell. His breathing had quickened, and he thrashed in the confines of the narrow bed while his closed eyelids fluttered erratically. His lips moved without sound. Without warning, he bolted upright and screamed.

The undiluted anguish in his cry wrenched Ren to her feet. She buzzed the lock and ran for the hold to throw the door open. Once inside, she stopped three feet from the bunk, unsure what to do next.

He didn't seem to notice her presence. Before she could determine her next step, the station door opened to admit Brady and Desmond—who both stopped abruptly when they saw what was going on.

"Bowers, get the hell out of there!" Brady drew his gun and charged across the room. Desmond followed at his heels. Ren was too shocked to protest as they pushed her out of the cell.

"We told you this guy is dangerous," Brady said. Replacing the piece to pull out his club, he turned his attention on the prisoner, who sat rigid and staring at nothing. Brady advanced on him. "You asshole. What'd you say to get her in here?"

The crack of the stick jolted Ren into focus. "Brady, stop!" she cried, further horrified when the victim of Brady's abuse thumped to the floor. "He didn't say anything. I just—it seemed like he was in distress."

Sneering, Brady lashed out with a foot and kicked the downed man. "He *oughta* be in distress," he said over the pained grunt that drifted upward. "He *should* be feeling guilty enough to make sure he never sleeps again." Brady leaned down close to the guy's face. "Or maybe even enough to confess. How 'bout it, Tyrell? You ready to give up yet?"

"You...wish..."

With a snarl, Brady dropped the club, lifted the prisoner and dragged him across the floor to slam him into the bars. He let go, and watched with satisfaction as the man slid to the ground, then leaned over, palms flat to the cell wall, and started kicking over and over.

"Brady!" Ren lurched toward the cell door, but Desmond stepped up and blocked the entrance. While Brady continued to pummel the fallen prisoner, Desmond said, "Don't try to butt in. The guy deserves it—and if you're not on our side, you're on his. Know what I mean...rookie?"

Ren looked from the stern visage in front of her to the crumpled wreck off to the side. The man didn't utter a sound through the vicious beating, and when Brady finally stepped back, Desmond said, "My turn."

"You can't do this." Ren tried to push past Brady as he changed places with Desmond. "You don't have anything on him. He's not resisting. Damn it, he can't even stand up!" She flinched when Desmond caught the vagrant in the shin, eliciting a sharp groan from the curled form at his feet.

Brady surged forward, forcing Ren to stumble back from the hold. Wedged in the opening, he said, "Attempted assault on an officer. We've got just cause."

"He wasn't attempting to assault me," Ren replied. She used slow, deliberate tones, since Brady apparently hadn't understood her the first time. "He sat up and screamed. I went in to make sure he wasn't in need of medical attention." She glared contempt at Brady. "Guess he is now, though."

"I think we have ourselves a misunderstanding here, Bowers." Grinning, he tossed a quick nod at Desmond, who hauled the prisoner to his knees and backhanded him.

"Desmond. Let him go." Shock stole the force from her demand, and her words emerged a whispered plea.

Brady laughed. "Who's gonna make him?"

Available at Wild Child Publishing.com.